Wendy S. Marcus is not a lifelong reader. As a child she never burrowed under her covers with a flashlight and a good book. In senior English she skimmed the classics, reading the bare minimum required to pass the class. Wendy found her love of reading later in life, in a box of old paperbacks at a school fundraiser where she was introduced to the romance genre in the form of a Harlequin Superromance. Since that first book she's been a voracious reader of romance—oftentimes staying up way too late in order to reach the happy ending before letting herself go to sleep.

Wendy lives in the beautiful Hudson Valley region of New York, with her husband, two of their three children, and their beloved dog Buddy. A nurse by trade, Wendy has a Master's degree in healthcare administration. After years of working in the medical profession she's taken a radical turn to write hot, contemporary romances with strong heroes, feisty heroines and lots of laughs. Wendy loves hearing from readers. Please visit her blog at www.WendySMarcus.com

Recent titles by the same author:

THE NURSE'S NOT-SO-SECRET SCANDAL
ONCE A GOOD GIRL…
WHEN ONE NIGHT ISN'T ENOUGH

These ~~titles are also available in eBook format~~

This book is dedicated to Army Specialist Adam Bivins
and to men and women around the world
who risk their lives to fight for the freedom of others.

With special thanks to:

My wonderful editor, Flo Nicoll, for believing in me and
always helping me find my way when I veer off track.

My supportive husband, for calling from work at the end
of each day to ask what he should pick up for dinner.

My three loving children,
for making me proud of the wonderful people
they are growing up to be. I am truly blessed.

BEYOND THE SPOTLIGHT
Uncovering the real Piermont sisters…

Identical twin nurses Jaci and Jena Piermont
grew up in society's limelight but their
glittering lifestyle hides dark secrets—
money has *never* bought them love.

What these reluctant socialites want are men
who can see past their wealth to the real
women beneath…but they'll have to be very
special to deserve these sisters!

In **CRAVING HER SOLDIER'S TOUCH**
feisty Jaci comes face-to-face with
a man from her past—
and he's as dangerously delicious as ever!

Shy Jena is reunited with the father
of her twins in
SECRETS OF A SHY SOCIALITE…
but what will happen when he discovers
her greatest secret of all?

Sexy, glamorous and emotionally powerful—

don't miss this thrilling new duet
by Wendy S. Marcus!

Dear Reader

After spending so many months writing the three books in my *Madrin Memorial Hospital* series, it was difficult to move on from the familiar characters I'd grown to love like family—especially with reader requests for books on Dr Starzi and Polly. Maybe some day. For those of you who know me, you know I am not a fan of change. Yet I make every effort to embrace it because I realise with change comes new opportunities, growth and—dare I admit?—a bit of excitement in trying something new.

So, with an encouraging nudge from my lovely editor, Flo Nicoll, I set out to create two new stories surrounding Jaci and Jena Piermont, identical twin nurses and members of New York's social elite. With Jaci's story I delved into home healthcare, abused women, and PTSD—post-traumatic stress disorder. With Jena's story I explored BRCA genetic testing for breast cancer, treatment options for those positive for the genetic mutation, and the impact of both on a single mother determined to live for her daughters.

As I began to write it didn't take long for me to fall in love with Jaci and Jena—two strong women who, each in their own way, overcome family tragedy to triumph as adults. And now they are both a welcome addition to the family of characters already established in my mind.

I hope you enjoy reading Jaci and Jena's stories as much as I enjoyed writing them.

To learn more about me, or my *Madrin Memorial Hospital* series, please visit my website: http://WendySMarcus.com

Wishing you all good things

Wendy S. Marcus

CRAVING
HER SOLDIER'S
TOUCH

BY
WENDY S. MARCUS

First published in Great Britain 2013
by Mills & Boon, an imprint of Harlequin (UK) Limited.
Harlequin (UK) Limited, Eton House, 18-24 Paradise Road,
Richmond, Surrey TW9 1SR

© Wendy S. Marcus 2013

ISBN: 978 0 263 23345 2

Harlequin (UK) policy is to use papers that are natural, renewable and recyclable products and made from wood grown in sustainable forests. The logging and manufacturing process conform to the legal environmental regulations of the country of origin.

Printed and bound in Great Britain
by CPI Antony Rowe, Chippenham, Wiltshire

PROLOGUE

IAN CALVIN EDDELTON, aka Ice to his army ranger buddies, looked up at the vision of blonde-haired, blue-eyed, bare-skinned loveliness now straddling his naked thighs, her palms pushing down on his pecs, forcing his back into the plush sheets of her bed. As if a tiny thing like her could hold him down if he didn't *want* to be held down.

"You don't have to do this." He forced out the words despite his brain's best rationalizations to suppress them. A fun bout of banter turned sexual challenge had never resulted in either of them shedding their clothes before. He needed her to be sure.

Beautiful, determined eyes met his. "Yes. I do."

Looked like the woman who didn't want sex to ruin their friendship, and the man who didn't want friendship to ruin their sex, were both about to get screwed. Literally.

He caressed the smooth skin of her perfect ass, usually hidden by a pair of skimpy running shorts or some fitted designer duds, and eased her closer to Ian junior who stood tall, sheathed, and eager to explore her internal terrain. To learn the secrets of what gave her pleasure and exploit them until she screamed his name over and over. Like he'd bragged he could on their many long runs rife with blatant flirtation and sexual innuendo.

But, "Why?" Why tonight, of all nights, when he'd been trying to lure her into bed for months, when by this time tomorrow he'd be on a plane headed back to the war in Iraq?

She smiled. Damn she was beautiful. "Consider it my bit to support our troops."

Tease.

Ian ran his fingers along the outside of her firm thighs. "There are thousands of us." Rounded her hips, followed the curve of her narrow waist, up to her ribs. "You do this sort of thing often?" He slid his thumbs across her taut nipples.

She trembled.

"You," she lowered her luscious breasts to his chest and leaned close to his ear, "are lucky number one." She rocked her hips until she had him poised at her entrance.

The urge to tell her there'd better not be a number two, that she should mail out brownies and holiday cards instead, came out of nowhere. Because she could do whatever the hell she wanted. They weren't going together, would never be anything more than friends— although an ongoing friends with benefits type deal was looking mighty appealing from where he lay. Hooah.

He tilted his pelvis, gave her a small taste of what was to come. "So it turns out you're a sucker for a man in uniform after all."

"I'm a sucker for *you*, Staff Sergeant," she whispered, circling the perimeter of his inner ear with her tongue, sending rippling waves of arousal throughout his body. "And when you're lying on your cot in the dead of night, exhausted, your mind reeling from the events of the day, I want to be your oasis in the desert,

the calm that relaxes you before you drift off to sleep."
She lifted her upper body, shifted her hips, and took
him deep. "I want you to think about us. Like this."

Getting himself to *stop* thinking about them like this
was going to be the problem.

She rode him slowly, their eyes locked, their bodies
in total sync. "I want you to fight hard and stay safe
and look forward to the day I will welcome you home.
Just. Like. This." She punctuated each of her last three
words with a swift thrust of her hips before collapsing
onto his chest, sliding her hands around his sides and
hugging him. "I'm going to miss you."

An odd sensation squeezed his heart. At the same
time, an unsettling concoction churned in his gut.

Could it be guilt? Because, to avoid a protracted,
teary goodbye, he would slip away as soon as she fell
asleep.

Maybe remorse? Because he'd gone overseas and
returned home enough times over the past ten years
to know nothing ever remained the same. By the time
he came home she'd probably be settled on one of the
well-bred, successful business associates her brother
seemed hell-bent on fixing her up with.

Or a hint of longing for what he could not have? Because he was career military and refused to put any
woman through what his mother had suffered as the
spouse of an active duty soldier.

Nah. A simple case of agita from his double order
of farewell steak fajitas made more sense, since Ian
Eddelton did not succumb to emotion. Ever. On the
battlefield, emotion, distraction of any kind, gave an
enemy the advantage, and got good men and women
killed. On a personal level, emotion made men weak
and vulnerable. Never again.

Ian flipped Jaci onto her back and took control, pushing all thoughts from his mind except how unbelievably amazing she felt beneath him, surrounding him, and how he was going to spend the next few hours in heaven…before he returned to hell.

CHAPTER ONE

Almost thirteen months later

SOMETHING had gone wrong.

Two male thug-looking types in dark baggy pants and oversized sweatshirts exited the rear door of the rundown, graffiti ridden brick building. Community health nurse and Women's Crisis Center advocate Jaci Piermont slid further down in the front seat of the clunker she'd borrowed from the center, trying to melt into the darkness. Even in broad daylight, when entering Nap Tower to visit her patients, Jaci never came unaccompanied, and never went near the rear door, a known hangout for drug dealers and troublemakers of every variety.

But tonight it was raining. Pouring actually. The beginnings of a hurricane expected to slam the northeast coast of the U.S., Westchester County in its projected path. They'd specifically chosen this night figuring no one would be outside.

Jaci's phone rang.

She checked the number. Carla. Assistant Director of the Women's Crisis Center.

"Hey," Jaci said, peering out the bottom portion of the driver's side window.

"You were due here twenty minutes ago," Carla demanded.

"She didn't show." She being Merlene K., twenty-five-year-old white female in need of assistance to escape a controlling/abusive relationship with the father of her unborn child. No local friends or family willing to intervene.

"Get out of there, Jaci. You can't help her if she doesn't follow the plan."

That they'd been working on for weeks. "Everything was set." Every detail worked out with their contact who resided in the building. Merlene's boyfriend's work schedule checked and verified and rechecked. His accomplice, who kept an eye on Merlene while he worked the night shift, distracted. A duffel for her meager belongings. A change of clothes and a wig so she could alter her appearance and slip away unnoticed.

The door opened again. "Oh no," Jaci said.

"What's happening?"

"It's Merlene. She's not alone." In the one working light over the door, through the blur of the rain spattered window, Jaci could still make out Merlene's battered face, and that of her bastard boyfriend, pure evil, gripping her arm tightly in one hand, dragging her, carrying a stuffed duffel Jaci recognized as the one she'd dropped off last week, in the other.

Merlene shuffled behind him, hunched over, her right arm clutching her abdomen. Damn him.

Jaci straightened her short, bob-styled black wig, pushed in her false teeth, and adjusted her faux eyeglasses.

The couple was approximately twenty feet away, walking in her direction.

"Do not get out of that car," Carla cautioned.

"She needs medical attention," Jaci whispered as if they could hear her. "Who knows where he's taking her, if we'll ever have another opportunity to help her."

Ten feet.

Jaci reached for the door handle.

"Do not—" Carla started.

"You'd better call Justin." She never did a pick-up in this area unless Justin was on duty. "Tell him to hurry."

Jaci ended the call. After a deep calming breath, she stuck the phone in the pocket of her black rain slicker, pulled the hood up over her head, and pushed open a door.

Rain pelted her in the face.

"Excuse me," she yelled.

Merlene jumped. Her boyfriend stopped and pulled the woman he treated as a possession, to do with as he chose, close.

"My car won't start," Jaci lied. "You got any jumper cables?" The wind tried to blow off her hood. She held it in place, thankful she'd remembered to slip on a pair of knit gloves to cover her manicure.

"No," the abuser said, and pulled Merlene away.

Please let Justin be on his way.

"Excuse me, miss," Jaci said to Merlene. "Are you okay?"

"She's fine," a deep, irritated voice snapped. He didn't bother to look back at her.

"I'm sorry. But she doesn't look fine. Maybe I can…"

Merlene turned around, squinted against the raindrops, and studied her face. "Ja…"

Jaci shook her head, warning Merlene not to use her real name. "Are you in need of assistance, miss?" Jaci yelled over the wind.

"Mind your own business," the large man all but

growled, jerking to a stop beside a shiny new black SUV almost glowing in the overhead light. While his girlfriend, the mother of his unborn child, couldn't afford maternity clothes, was forced to wait hours at the free clinic for prenatal care, and wandered the building offering to clean apartments and do odd jobs to earn money for food.

Which is how Jaci had learned of her.

Where the heck was Justin?

Merlene's boyfriend released her long enough to open the rear door of his vehicle. And that's all it took. With a look of absolute panic she lunged at Jaci, clamping her arms tightly behind Jaci's neck. "Don't let him take me," she cried out.

Jaci slid her left arm around Merlene's waist and plunged her right hand into her pocket to retrieve the canister of pepper spray she'd placed there earlier. "You are not going anywhere without me," Jaci said. Meaning it. Prepared to do anything within her power to keep Merlene safe.

The first blow struck Jaci in the left posterior ribs, an intense, stabbing pain only minimally less severe than the closed-fisted punch to the right upper arm that felt like it shattered her proximal humerus.

The pepper spray clattered on the asphalt.

He was strong. Angry. And not wasting his time with words.

Well, Jaci was no stranger to the pain of abuse. And if Merlene could deal with it day after day, Jaci could put up with it until Justin arrived. She wound her other arm around Merlene's waist, locking her fingers together, and took a stand.

"Don't hit her," Merlene pleaded, releasing Jaci, trying to push her away.

"No." Jaci tried to hold on. The over-sized bully grabbed her by the wrists, wrenched her hands apart, and pushed her to the side in the same manner he'd probably treat a pesky toddler. The force made her stumble. Her heel caught the edge of a huge pothole filled with water and she went down with a splash. Both hands slapped the cracked, pebble-ridden pavement. Stung. Pain shot through her right arm, which gave out.

Merlene screamed.

The flashing lights of a police cruiser lit up the sky, its headlights illuminating Jaci where she lay.

She tried to get up. "Stay down," Justin yelled, running from his vehicle. His weapon drawn, aimed at Merlene's boyfriend. "Release her," Justin ordered.

Once free, Merlene ran to Jaci and dropped to the ground beside her. "I'm sorry. So sorry," she cried.

"It's not your fault," Jaci said, putting her left arm around Merlene's shoulders. "You're safe now."

Another car sped into the parking lot.

Carla ran toward them. "Are you okay?"

"How did you get here so fast?" Jaci asked.

"When you didn't show up on time I thought you were in trouble. I was already on my way when I called."

And that's why she loved Carla. "Merlene needs medical treatment," Jaci said.

"What about you?"

"I'm fine. Sore, but fine."

"Let me help you," a vaguely familiar masculine voice offered as large hands grabbed her from behind and lifted her to standing position.

Jaci couldn't control a yelp of pain at the pressure on the exact spot where she'd been punched minutes earlier.

"I'm sorry," he said, releasing her. "I didn't mean—"

"You are not fine," Carla yelled.

"He hit her," Merlene sobbed. "Her arm might be broken."

"That son of a bitch hit you?" the man asked with rage in his voice.

"Nothing's broken. See." She lifted her arm overhead and across her chest, despite the pain, to prove to Carla she was fine.

"Stay here." The man stormed over to Justin who yelled, "I told you to stay in the car."

That's when recognition dawned. The broad shoulders filling out his dark windbreaker. The confident stride, camouflage pants and short military-style haircut.

Another one-two punch, this one invisible, knocked the wind from her lungs.

Ian Eddelton.

A good friend and, when he was in town, an occasional roommate of Justin's, making him her on-again, off-again upstairs neighbor. He'd been her good friend, too, or so she'd thought. Until she'd thrown sex and the word 'marriage' into the mix and he'd run like she'd asked for a kidney donation then whipped out a salad fork and a steak knife intending to harvest the organ right there on her bed.

That was the last time she'd seen or spoken to him, supporting her brother's claim that no man in his right mind would willingly marry her without a monetary incentive. Men wanted her money and/or her body, but no one wanted her.

Jerk.

Jaci wiped the rain from her face. "I'm going home," she said to Carla. "I'll stop by the center tomorrow to exchange cars."

Carla touched her wrist gently. "Are you sure you don't need an X-ray?"

"I'm sure." Even if she did, she wouldn't go to the hospital now, couldn't risk anyone recognizing her or associating her name with an actual crisis center rescue. Because anonymity kept her safe. Because socialites on the fundraising circuit didn't dirty their hands with actual in-the-trenches work. Because Jerald X. Piermont III would have an absolute hissy-fit if his wayward sister wound up in the online gossip blogs. Again.

Knowing Carla would see to Merlene, and Justin would see to Merlene's butt of a boyfriend, Jaci headed for the car. Suddenly chilled, she needed to get home to warm up with a hot bath and a cup of tea.

She wrapped her arms around her middle to contain a shaky, uneasy feeling.

"Funny," Ian said from behind her. "I never took you for the type to slink off under the cover of darkness."

"No. That's your M.O." She picked up her pace.

"I told Justin I'd drive you home," he said, ignoring her retort. "He'll stop by your place tomorrow to take your statement of what happened."

She turned on him. "Why are you here?"

"Justin asked me to bring him some dry clothes down at the station. I was there when your friend called." He held out his hand. "Give me your keys."

Home from Iraq for at least three weeks and it'd taken a coincidence and a call for help to get him to talk to her? "Go to hell." Jaci turned, took the last few steps to the car, and opened the door.

Ian stopped her from climbing in with a gentle hand on her waist which he used to ease her back into his chest. "I've already been there," he said just loud enough for her to hear. "I'm sorry I left the way I did."

No one was sorrier than Jaci.

Because Ian Eddelton had turned out to be a slug who'd slimed all over any hope she'd had for a palatable solution to the kiss-her-new-husband-or-kiss-her-trust-fund-goodbye dilemma. And the deadline for 'I dos' was fast approaching.

Ian held her close, relieved she was okay, mad as hell she'd come to this area alone, put herself in danger. He'd seen the horrors, the atrocities. Women beaten, raped, and worse.

"You're hurting me," Jaci cried out, trying to twist out of his hold on her.

Ian turned her to face him. "What the hell were you thinking? Coming here at night. Alone. You could have been—"

"But I wasn't. Now let go of me."

"What if Justin wasn't available when your friend called?" He held her tighter. "What if he was miles away from here? What if he had no cell service?"

She sucked in a breath and winced in pain.

He'd forgotten how delicate she was. "I'm sorry."

"It's not your fault." She looked away.

Rage flowed through his system, the urge to beat that miscreant in Justin's custody so bad he was incapable of ever raising a hand to a woman again was hard to contain. "Where else did he hit you?"

She didn't answer.

He scooped her into his arms, with the utmost care, and carried her to the passenger door. "When I get you home I'm going to strip off your clothes and examine every inch of you." Objectively. Impersonally. With complete focus on his mission: To identify injury and evaluate for need of medical treatment. Oh, who the hell was he trying to kid?

"You'll have to knock me unconscious to do it." She struggled to get free.

"The only place you're going is from my arms into that car seat. Now hand me the keys because I'm wet and angry and not in the mood to get shot or knifed by any of the scumbags who frequent this neighborhood."

She gave him the keys.

As he slid her into the car he gave into the urge and whispered, "For the record, I'm not a fan of the new look." If he hadn't known it was Jaci, he never would have recognized her.

"Good," she snapped. "First thing tomorrow I'll make it permanent."

He closed the door and smiled, remembered the stimulating, entertaining banter between them, the companionship, friendship and lust, and felt almost normal. But since his return from Iraq, his life had been anything but.

After adjusting the driver's seat to accommodate his six foot, probably down to one hundred and eighty-five-pound frame, Ian turned the key in the ignition and the old car sputtered to life. "This is your choice for a getaway car?" Thing probably wouldn't reach fifty miles per hour without a good push and the benefit of a downward slope.

"It's not like I was robbing a bank." Jaci turned to look out the window, her arms crossed tightly over her chest. "It blends in," she added quietly.

Yeah. More than her little red BMW would.

Ian turned right out of the parking lot. A few more turns and he was on the highway heading home. A tense quiet filled the car broken only by the rapid slap of the windshield wipers. Most definitely not the kind of quiet the shrink at the rehab had recommended. A bomb blast echoed in the deep recesses of his mind.

Not now.

He imagined Jaci chatting. The way she spoke so fast and used her hands when she got excited. The melodic fluctuations in her tone. The movement of her sensual lips. Her smile. The way she elbowed him or punched him when he made a snide comment or teased her.

The yelling of soldiers filled his ears. Chaos. *"Medic. I need a medic over here!"*

Deep breath. *Keep it together Ice.*

Focus.

He searched for something to say, to keep him in the present, and homed in on the first thing that came to mind. "Do you have a death wish or something? Showing up at the most dangerous housing complex in the south side of Mount Vernon, in the dark, alone. It was a total rookie move. One that could have gotten you killed." He tightened his grip on the steering wheel to keep from reaching over to shake some sense into her. Anger boiled deep in his gut. *Not good.* Convincing wealthy benefactors to part with their cash in support of her crisis center was where she belonged. Not on the front line, dealing with reprobates and confronting danger.

His heart pounded. A trickle of sweat wove its way down his temple.

"I'll have you know I've been doing this for three years," she said, "since I started the Women's Crisis Center. And I have never run into a problem until tonight."

Three years? "Pure dumb luck." His heart skipped a

beat. "At some point your luck will run out." Just like his had. He wanted to hit something. "Did Justin know?"

"As of tonight he does," she said.

"This woman, the one you set out to rescue tonight. She's so special her safety is worth putting yours at risk?"

"You don't know anything about me, do you?" she asked.

He knew everything that mattered. She was smart, funny, thoughtful, beautiful, sexy, and there was a time he'd rather spend his time with her than with anyone else.

She shifted in her seat to face him. "Come on, Ian. Tell the truth. You never looked me up on the Internet? Never gave in to that niggling interest people seem to have about just how much I'm worth?"

Eyes focused on the road, he shook his head. "Sorry to disappoint but I prefer to get to know people on my own terms rather than reading what others have to say about them, and I'm more interested in your body than your bank account." Was interested. Was, as in past tense. He could not allow Jaci to distract him from what he had to do.

She smiled. "You always tell it like it is, don't you?"

He glanced over and smiled right back. "That's why you love me."

Her smile vanished.

Wrong thing to say. Idiot. Because she didn't love him. At the moment she barely liked him, her scorn totally justified. It was for the best, for both of them. That didn't mean he had to like it.

He waited for her to lay into him.

Instead she said, "When you get home tonight, go online and keyword Piermont Tragedy, Scarsdale, New

York. Then you'll understand why I will do whatever I can to help women escape abusive relationships. And since I'm of legal age, no one gets a say in how I go about doing it." She turned back toward the window. "This conversation is over."

In the interest of peace between them, he let the topic slide. "I, uh, got your letter." Perfectly formed cursive written on classy pale pink stationery in purple ink. Five pages front and back, upbeat, with no mention of her proposal of marriage or his rude, hasty retreat. The woman could make the simple act of doing laundry entertaining. And the scent. Her perfume. He'd stored it in a zipper-lock plastic bag to preserve the aroma, carried it in his pocket, slept with it, jerked off to it.

"If you'd left me a way to contact you before you took off, if you'd put forth the slightest effort by writing me back or e-mailing me or in some way letting me know it got to you, maybe I would have sent you more." She spoke without moving, still looking out the window. But the emotion in her voice let him know he'd hurt her feelings.

So much for peace between them.

He tried to explain. "When I'm in a warzone I can't be distracted by thoughts of home. I'm there to do a job, to complete the tasks I'm assigned and get out alive." He glanced at her. "And I thought it'd be easier on you to not feel obligated to write me or think about me." Or worry or search for lists of dead and wounded every time a bloody battle made the news. Like his mother had each time his father had been deployed overseas.

"So let me get this straight." She turned to him and finally took off that ridiculous wig. "For the better part of four months we spent a portion of almost every day together. I ran with you."

He'd timed his runs to make sure he'd pass by their parking lot at exactly six o'clock to facilitate their meeting up for the last five miles of his ten mile jog.

"I cooked for you."

His mouth watered at the memory of her chicken with rosemary.

"We watched movies on my couch."

His body ached to feel her cuddled up beside him.

"Our friendship progressed to the point I invited you into my bed, into my body, into my future. And in that feeble-minded head of yours you came to the conclusion if you fled my condo—in your boxer shorts you were in such a hurry—then scurried off to the base hours before you were scheduled to report and cut off all contact with me I would poof," she flared out her fingers in front of her beautiful face, "forget all about you?"

Or hate him. Either way, a clean break.

"Maybe your attempt would have been more successful," she went on, "if you hadn't stolen from me. If each time I looked at the shelves in my living room I wasn't reminded that the empty space where my favorite picture of Jena and me is supposed to be is empty because of *you*." She crossed her arms over her chest. "All you had to do was ask, and I'd have happily given you a picture."

But it may not have been the one he'd wanted. Jaci and her identical twin, standing arm in arm by what looked like the family swimming pool, wearing matching string bikinis so skimpy they wouldn't have passed for bathing suits on most public U.S. beaches.

And had he asked to take a picture of her with him to war, she would have thought there was more to their relationship than there was. Or than he'd thought there was at the time.

Would she be less angry if he'd ripped the photo down the center and only taken the half with her in it? Because as much as he'd wanted to make a clean break, he couldn't get himself to leave without having some piece of her to hold on to, and one glimpse of the snapshot in the light and he could tell the twins apart.

Jaci's smile warm and genuine. Her eyes lit with laughter, fun, and mischief. Her sister's smile shy almost forced. Cautious. Her eyes haunted and sad.

"Maybe if someone hadn't e-mailed my brother and a dozen or so other men in our social circle that some soldier in Iraq was bragging about a threesome he'd had with me and Jena. God." She threw the wig in a bag at her feet. "The thought repulses me. You repulse me."

Ian fought for calm as he leaned out the window to punch in his code, waited for the metal gates to open and steered the car into the parking lot of their luxury high rise. "I never said that, Jaci. I swear."

"Were we or were we not referred to as Ice melt?" she yelled. "That's your nickname, isn't it? Ice?"

Ian parked the car in Jaci's spot, turned off the engine, and shifted to face her. "I didn't tell anyone you, Jena and I had sex together." He ran a hand over his face. Disgusted. "Guys are pigs. Get a bunch of them together on a military base, add in a picture of two, identical, hot, almost naked women, and it was the twin fantasy run amok."

Apparently he was going about this explanation thing all wrong because Jaci thrust open her car door and jumped out like the interior of the vehicle had caught fire.

"Wait," he called out, rushing through the rain, his left leg stiff, slowing him down. "I didn't say it was *my* fantasy." Well. Okay. To be perfectly honest the thought had crossed his mind—briefly—when they'd first met. But since honesty didn't seem to be working out so well for him at the moment, he decided to keep that bit of truth to himself.

Bottom line, a few days in Jaci's company and he'd had no desire to share their limited time together with anyone else. Male or female.

He caught up to her as she was scanning her key card in front of the security sensor. With a buzz the door unlocked and Ian opened it. In the vestibule he pushed on the inner glass door to stop her from entering the lobby. She wouldn't look at him.

"In all the years my squad has known me, I have never once tacked up a picture on my locker," he explained to the back of her head. Or gotten caught staring at one like some homesick teenager, unprepared for how much he'd miss her or how the idea of having a beautiful wife to return home to would start to appeal to him. "They made a big deal of it and things got way out of hand. You have to know I would never disrespect you by discussing anything that went on in private between us. And I would never disparage your or your sister's reputation by spreading lies. I had no idea the rumors made their way back to the U.S. until I returned home and Justin told me."

"My face is in the newspaper at least twice a month. You didn't consider the possibility someone might recognize me?"

No. He hadn't. "It's a different world over there. I'll talk to your brother." Had already left four messages at his office requesting an appointment. "I'll make a statement to the press."

Jaci looked at him like he'd offered to don a pink tutu and tights. "Don't you dare. All that will do is stir the whole thing up again and bring out the whack-a-dos who corroborated the stories and made up lies about Jena and me dating back to junior high school. Now if you don't mind, I'm wet and tired and would like to slip into a hot bath and put this night behind me."

At the thought of a naked Jaci, her slick body surrounded by bubbles, submerged in a candlelit tub, Ian felt the twinges of life return to Ian junior.

Ah, yes. Half an hour in Jaci's presence provided Ian with glimpses of the man he'd been before the explosion, a man capable of feeling more than the anguish of regret, guilt, and loss, something weeks of therapy hadn't been able to do. He opened the door and followed her through.

In the elevator she pressed the buttons for the fourth and fifth floors. He broke the uncomfortable silence by offering his most sincere apology, "I'm sorry." Because he was.

She let out a breath and looked down at her black rain boots. "I'm glad you made it home safely." The doors opened on the fourth floor. She took a step forward, and, standing between them she looked back at him and said, "But what's done is done. It's over. Leave it alone."

He exited the elevator and followed her. God help him, he didn't want it to be over. Which was why night after night he'd fought the urge to bang on her door, to explain why he'd run, to apologize for what he'd said, and beg her forgiveness.

But to what end?

He trailed behind her.

No matter how much he may have wanted to explore the possibility of a future with Jaci, the bomb blast that'd killed his men obliterated all possibility of a happily ever after for Ian. She'd never understand or accept what he had to do. What woman would? And the last thing he needed was one more person preaching to him about survivor guilt and overreaction due to grief and mourning. Few people understood the bonds formed in battle when soldiers entrusted their lives to the members of their team. The vow—spoken or unspoken—to look after a brother's family should he be unable to do it himself. There was nothing Ian wouldn't do for his men—overseas or stateside. And nothing they wouldn't do for him.

If they were still alive.

But they weren't. So it fell to Ian, the last man standing, to look after their wives and children, so they weren't left to struggle like Ian, his mother and sisters had after his father's death. To preserve their memory, honor their dedication to their country, and make sure no one tried to suppress, diminish or taint either out of anger, resentment or feelings of abandonment, like his mother had.

Their children would grow up with a man around. Ian. Not their fathers, but the next best thing. Their children would grow up knowing their fathers loved them and fought to make the future safer. For them. Their children would be allowed to remain children because Ian would do his best to fill the role of man-around-the-house.

For four households.

His life was no longer his own and the stress of the responsibility he'd taken on and the promises he'd made weighed heavily on his already overburdened psyche.

He'd reached his limit, could not deal with one more woman, one more responsibility in his life. And yet, seeing Jaci again, feeling her, remembering carefree times, Ian couldn't bear the thought of leaving her, of returning to his condo. Alone. To the nightmares that awaited him whenever he closed his eyes. To the anxiety and tension and overall feeling of instability that plagued him since his return.

She stopped at her door.

His heart pounded. His chest grew tight. Sweat pooled in his armpits.

"Please," he said. God help him he was begging her to let him stay in her presence, to keep him from retreating into the dark, torturous depths of his mind.

She took out her key. "You are not coming in."

Desperation gripped him. Panic.

She unlocked the door and opened it.

A baby cried out from inside, clearing his head instantly.

Ian stood in shock unable to move.

Jaci had a baby? No way she'd been pregnant before they'd slept together. He'd monopolized every moment of her spare time for the four months beforehand. Could she have fallen into another man's arms so soon after his deployment? Maybe. But not likely. Jaci teased and flirted. A lot. But she was very selective about who shared her bed, at least according to Justin who'd known her since high school.

It was one of the reasons their night together meant so much.

Which had to mean the baby was his.

Taking advantage of his stupor, she escaped inside, closing the door behind her.

Ian leaned up against the wall, his mouth suddenly dry, swallowing difficult. He was a man teetering on the edge of sanity, a man with no viable means to support himself, or replenish the savings he'd already spent to fulfill his commitment to his fallen brothers.

And now he was a father, responsible for a tiny, defenseless baby, in addition to everything else.

A baby no one had bothered to tell him about.

Justin was a dead man.

CHAPTER TWO

"YOU'RE here! Three days early." Jaci's conflicting emotions over seeing Ian vanished, replaced by jubilation at the return of her sister. She tossed her bag on the kitchen counter, yanked off her raincoat, and toed off her boots.

"I tried to call your home phone when we arrived. Luckily Brandon was at the concierge desk," Jena said. "I didn't think you'd mind us coming right up."

"Of course not. How are you? How was your trip? Is everything okay?" She stripped off her wet clothes right there in the entryway, could not wait to hug her sister and meet her tiny, crying nieces.

"Why are you all wet?" Jena asked.

"Pick up for the crisis center." No sense worrying her sister with the details. In nothing but a tee and panties, Jaci charged across the hardwood floor of her living room in bare feet. "You look fabulous." A little white lie. She pulled her twin into her arms and squeezed her tight. "I missed you so much. Promise me you're home to stay." Her eyes filled with tears.

Jena hugged her back with equal vigor. "If you promise me that no matter what happens you won't hate me."

Hate her? "Are you kidding me?" Jaci tightened her hold. "I could never, ever hate you. I love you." She stepped back. "Look at these adorable babies." She rubbed her cold hands together. "I need to wash my hands and warm up before I touch them. Brrrrr it's chilly in here."

"Only if you're wet and naked."

"So I'm not complaining or anything." Jaci hurried down the hallway to her bathroom. "But what's with the surprise arrival?"

"I was worried about the weather. They're predicting heavy flooding all along the east coast from the storm, and I didn't want to miss the charity ball," Jena called after her.

"So you can protect me from Jerry Three?" Since she'd stopped responding to all communication from the current head of the family—despite his threats—after that horrible night he'd received the e-mail from Iraq and summoned her to the estate. Where he'd proceeded to unload every negative, hateful thought he'd harbored against her. It'd taken over an hour, during which he'd blocked her exit from his office. And he'd ended his tirade with a smack to the side of the head she hadn't seen coming.

Her own fault for underestimating his anger and overestimating how much he'd changed since she'd moved out.

"That's Jerald Xavier Piermont the third." Jena did an impressive impression of their pompous half-brother, a man who'd turned out exactly like the heavy-handed, business-focused, wealth-obsessed father they shared. "You disobedient, classless twit."

"You've been practicing." Jaci smiled, slid into her soft fleece robe and tied the sash. It was good to have her sister home. Where she belonged regardless of the secrets she kept. Like where she'd been for the past ten months, why she'd disappeared without a word of warning, and whose genetic contribution was partly responsible for her precious babies.

"He had the nerve to show up here two weeks ago," Jaci said. Uninvited. Unwelcome. To demand she stop her childish silent treatment and agree to a date with 'the most eligible bachelor in the tri-state area' who Jerry had convinced to meet her. And if she could pretend to be nice for a few short weeks, marriage would unite two powerful families and solidify a highly profitable business merger.

Jaci was not a bargaining chip.

"You know he isn't as bad as you make him out to be," Jena said.

Maybe not, if you were sweet and accommodating and easily influenced like Jena. Jaci washed her hands in hot water. But if you, heaven forbid, dared to question him or disagree with him or ignore one of his many ridiculous, oppressive rules, he could be—and was— brutal.

Jaci returned to the second bedroom which she'd outfitted as a nursery in preparation for the twins' arrival. "So if he's not so bad," Jaci said quietly. "Why didn't you stick around and have the babies locally?"

Without looking up, Jena snapped the sleeper of the baby on the changing table and shrugged.

"He doesn't know, does he?" Jaci asked.

Still looking at the baby, Jena shook her head. "I figured it'd be best to tell him in front of witnesses." She looked up and smiled. "With my older, wiser, fearless sister by my side."

"Two is always better than one," Jaci repeated their mantra for dealing with Jerry's nonsense.

"In this case one to do chest compressions while the

other runs for the defibrillator after I inform Jerald he's an uncle to two illegitimate little Piermonts," Jena said.

"I call the defibrillator." Jaci held up her hand. And if she should happen to trip and sprain her ankle on the way to get it…oh well.

Jena handed Jaci the baby from the changing table and lifted the other twin from the double stroller.

Jaci cuddled her niece close, rubbed her cheek over fine silky hair, and inhaled the scent of baby shampoo and powder and sweet, loving innocence. "Which of my adorable, unhappy nieces is this?" She rubbed her tiny back in an attempt to calm her.

"For the time being, I dress Abbie in pink and Annie in yellow, until I can tell them apart."

"Promise me you won't let anyone label them." The quiet/sweet/shy one. The mouthy/wild/disrespectful one. Childhood labels were near impossible to outgrow no matter how much a person tried to change or improve.

Jena—who'd often complained of feeling stifled under the expectation of *her* labels—shook her head. "Promise."

After Jena changed Annie, Jaci followed her into the kitchen, noting she'd lost all her pregnancy weight and then some. In the bright light she looked drained. Exhausted. Well Jaci would fix that with good food, lots of loving care, and a much needed second pair of hands. "Mom would have liked you naming one of your twins Annie." After her.

Jena smiled sadly. "I know."

Jaci settled into a kitchen chair. "I can hold Annie, too, while you make the bottles." She held out her left hand. "After all, I can't be the favorite aunt if I come off looking like I'm playing favorites."

"They're all of four weeks old, Jaci." Jena put her

free hand on her hip and gave Jaci the give-me-a-break look. "And you're their only aunt."

Was she? Without knowing the father's identity, how could she be sure? Jaci reached for a yellow-socked foot. "Come on. You've been hogging them for weeks. Now it's my turn."

Jena placed Annie in Jaci's available arm and she gave her second little niece some loving. "I was trying to clear my schedule before you got here, so I'm on call this week and have to head out for work early tomorrow morning. And I've got a full schedule after that. Will you be okay alone?"

"We'll be fine," Jena said with a tired smile.

"You know I may have mentioned you were coming home with the twins to Mrs. Calvin up on seven."

Jena shot her an aggravated look. "I specifically asked you not to tell anyone."

"How was I supposed to find a quality babysitter, who we are not friends with and doesn't know Jerry, to babysit on Saturday night without telling them about the twins? She seems nice and always smiles at me when I see her. And she looks so sad sitting in the lobby after her grandchildren leave every Sunday. I wanted to cheer her up. Hey." Jaci snapped her fingers. "I bet she'd love to come down and give you a hand if you need it tomorrow. It'd be a good opportunity for you to get to know her and show her how you like things done. I'll leave her number on the refrigerator before I head out in the morning."

After lifting Annie and handing Jaci Abbie's bottle Jena smiled. "It's good to be home."

With each baby now voraciously sucking on her bottle, the room got suddenly quiet. "How long do you plan to stay?" Jaci couldn't stop herself from asking. The stress of the next three months, of Jerry intensifying his crusade to marry them off to two of his business associates by their birthday, would be so much easier to handle with Jena by her side.

"Twenty-five years old," Jena said, as usual, knowing the real question behind her question.

"It'd always seemed so far away." Jaci stood, had to move. "Damn, daddy. It wasn't enough to control our every move while he was alive. He has to do it from his grave." Which he wouldn't be in if not for Jaci. So many times she'd wished him dead. Death by car accident, bullet wound to the chest from random mugging, asphyxiation from some outrageously expensive food delicacy lodged in his airway. He probably died the way he did on purpose. So she'd be blamed. So she'd have to live with the guilt.

Abbie stirred in her arms. "Ssshhh." She rocked the tiny bundle. "No one will ever hurt you, sweetie," she whispered. "You or your sister. Not as long as Auntie Jaci is around."

Ian couldn't breathe. Something heavy lay across his chest. He tried to move. Couldn't. His left leg caught in a vice. On fire.

Something dripped on his chin. He wiped it away. Tried to focus through the darkness.

Heat.

Another drop hit his mouth. He tasted blood. What the…?

Gunfire. In the distance.

Ice reached for his M16. Found a body part instead.

What the hell happened?

More gunfire.

He struggled to get free.

The vacant, lifeless eyes of his buddy, The Kid,

stared at him from a blood drenched face. The picture of the man's wife and one-year-old daughter flashed.

The smell of fire. Burnt flesh. Death.

A baby cried. His baby. He could not die.

A hand touched his shoulder.

They would not take him prisoner. Ian tore his leg from its restraint, pushed at the mass crushing his chest, and twisted free. He tackled his attacker, the enemy, responsible for the death of his team. He raised his fist, inhaled, and smelled…her. Jaci. Felt her warm, willing body beneath him.

Ian junior perked up with interest.

Oh how he'd missed her, dreamed of her, aroused and undulating beneath him. He rocked his hips, needed her, to escape. To forget.

"Ian. Stop." Not the words he wanted to hear right now. Usually she was so happy to see him. So welcoming. "Wake up. Get off me." Instead of pulling him close, she pushed at his chest, sounding…angry.

He opened his eyes to the shadowed greys of an overcast early morning—the wind and rain from last night still raging outside. He lay on his side between Justin's sofa and coffee table, on the floor, partially sprawled over a fully clothed Jaci.

A skilled tactician, Ian quickly scrolled through his options.

1) Retreat with an apology
2) Engage with an explanation
3) Instigate with an accusation
4) Distract with arousal

Since, by his estimation, lucky number four held the greatest potential for a pleasurable outcome, and it seemed a shame to let his first hard-on in months go to waste, Ian leaned close and nuzzled Jaci's ear. "About time you got around to welcoming me home properly. Like you promised." He pulled her into his arms. "I've dreamed of holding you."—At least he had until the explosion had blown every happy thought from his head. No. He would not think about that night or the war or all that had been lost as a result of a roadside bomb. Not when he had Jaci—the real Jaci—within kissing distance. Not when he had the chance to bury himself deep inside of her one last time.

He slid a knee between her legs and shifted on top of her, resting his upper body on his elbows, settling his pelvis in between her thighs. "Of making love to you." He rocked the length of his erection along the seam of her slacks. "Being inside you is like visiting paradise." And Ian was in serious need of a vacation.

Jaci let out a shaky breath and softened beneath him. Excellent.

"I can't do this, Ian."

Not so excellent. But Ian never surrendered without a fight. "I know you want me as much as I want you." He could tell by the change in her breathing, the way she'd bent and opened her knees to accommodate him, and the tiny, almost unnoticeable up-tilt of her hips to give him better access. "You don't have to do a thing." He knew what she liked. Resting his weight on one elbow, he freed up his right hand to caress her breast and tease her tight nipple all while continuing his slow, calculated assault on her sex. He let out a deep, heavy, hot breath in her ear. "I can have us undressed and on our way to Pleasure Town in under a minute."

All he needed was the slightest indication of agreement. A smile.

A nod.

Anything.

"Except for last night," she said, sounding perturbed. "We haven't seen or spoken to each other in over a year. You've been home for at least three weeks without any attempt to talk to me. I walked into your condo to find you half wedged into the sofa, groaning as if you're in pain, and fighting to get free. You attacked me when I tried to wake you. And you think the next few minutes would be best spent having sex?"

He didn't answer immediately for fear that was a trick question. Because he was a guy who hadn't been with a woman in twelve months, three weeks, two days, and approximately twelve hours. Who, as a result of his current position had just returned to the rank of fully functioning male—and a great big hallelujah to that— who was a pair of sweatpants, a pair of slacks, and a pair of panties away from sweet, nightmare eradicating, ecstasy. So hell Y-E-S he thought the next few minutes, the next few hours, would be best spent having sex.

Jaci set her hands on his chest and gave a push. "Please, be the gentleman I know you are capable of being, and get off of me."

Even though the thoughts scrolling through his head and the urges surging through his body were anything but gentlemanly, Ian rolled to the side and Jaci stood.

"We need to talk," she said, straightening her sweater.

He'd rather gnaw on a handful of habaneros.

"Was our friendship all a ploy to get me into bed? Did we even have a friendship?" She crossed her arms over her chest and stared down at him. "At the time I'd thought we did. But now I'm not so sure." She shook her head. "The more I think about it, the more I can't help wondering if you invested hours of your time, being your most fun and entertaining self, for the sole purpose of charming me out of my panties."

Jaci's panties. The visual, pink and sheer, skimpy, with lace, and the tiniest of bows, had him wanting to peel off her clothes, oh so slowly, to get to them. In that instant, he'd have gladly bargained away a decade of his life for a chance to see her naked, to touch her and hold her close for a few undisturbed minutes. Hours. Days. Weeks. Months. Years.

Focus, Ian.

"Was I an item on a list?" She held up an imaginary pad and read from it. "Things to do before I deploy. Laundry." She made an air check. "Pack." Another air check. "Have sex with Jaci." Triple air check.

Yeah. That'd been an extraordinary night.

Ian's left leg throbbed so he opted to move up to the couch rather than stand. Elbows on his knees he stared at the ground. "No, you weren't some item on a list, and our friendship wasn't a ploy to get you into bed." It may have started off as one, but quickly transformed into the real thing. Maybe even something more. Not that it mattered now.

"Well you have an odd way of showing it. Friendship requires some degree of effort, Ian. A phone call. A card now and then. An e-mail. Look at me so I know you're listening."

She was talking so loud, how could he not listen? He looked up.

"While I can convince myself that my proposal shocked you into running, and I can let you off the hook for being incommunicado while you were in Iraq, you've been home for at least three weeks. If someone hadn't parked in my spot, forcing me into the visitors' lot, I wouldn't have seen your SUV. It's like you snuck back into town and hoped I wouldn't find out."

Exactly. His plan had been to strengthen up—mentally and physically—before finding a place of his own in closer proximity to the four separate houses he would soon start visiting weekly. He'd figured one month tops, which, added to the three months he'd been hospitalized, equaled four months his men's wives had been on their own, with him capable of little more than telephone and financial support.

He needed to get out there, to become more of a presence in their lives. It's what'd kept him from giving up during endless setbacks and complications, during hours of excruciating treatments and therapies.

An image of The Kid's baby daughter flashed.

Which reminded him. Jaci wasn't the only one with a reason to be angry. "So if you didn't come up for sex," he pushed off the sofa and stood, fighting a wince when pain shot down his leg. "Why *are* you here? Finally getting around to congratulating me on the birth of my baby?"

Jaci's jaw dropped open but no sound came out. No apology or explanation. She stood totally still, staring up at him, with a look of absolute shock on her face. "You—" She cleared her throat. "Who? When?"

Nice try. "Cut the crap, Jaci."

"You bastard." In a move that caught him, a decorated staff sergeant in the U.S. Army, completely off guard, she lunged forward and slapped his cheek.

What the…? He grabbed her hand.

"Who is she? A fellow soldier? While I was here wasting my time worrying about you, even after all the crap you pulled, you were sleeping around with another woman?" She sucked in a breath. "Or were you seeing her in the months before you left? While I was at work?"

The woman made no sense.

She fought him. "Let go of me."

This time he was ready and caught her up in a bear hold with no intention of releasing her until he figured out what the heck was going on. "I heard the baby. Last night. When I walked you to your door."

"The twins?" she asked.

Lord help him. Twins. He hadn't thought of that. Two of everything at the same time. Visits to the doctor. Boyfriends. Cars. College educations. The cartilage in his knees turned to pudding. And while he concentrated on remaining upright, on the verge of disgracing himself by collapsing to the floor, Jaci jammed the heel of her rubber boot on the top of his bare foot, escaped his weakened grip and started to chuckle.

"You thought —?" She laughed so hard she couldn't finish. "You thought—?" She doubled over, stumbled to the couch and plopped down. After about a minute of trying to regain her composure, Jaci inhaled a deep breath, pushed it out and asked. "You thought I had your baby?"

She made it sound like such a ridiculous assumption he decided not to answer.

Then all humor fled, and like she suddenly realized she'd been insulted, she got mad. "You honestly thought I wouldn't tell you if I'd gotten pregnant? That I wouldn't include you in the birth of our child or introduce you to your son or daughter at the first opportunity?"

Obviously he hadn't done a thorough job of thinking things through because Jaci was straightforward and not at all the type of woman to lie about a pregnancy.

"The babies you heard," she stood, "are my nieces. And I'd appreciate it if you didn't mention them to anyone because Jena doesn't want people to know she's back in town until this weekend."

"What's this weekend?"

"The second annual benefit gala for the Women's Crisis Center."

"Is that the ritzy shindig Justin's running security for on Saturday night?" Her brother was an outspoken supporter of the crisis center. Hmmmm... The perfect opportunity for a little man to poor-excuse-for-a-brother chat and to take care of the asses who'd been giving Jaci a hard time.

Jaci nodded. "This year we're having a silent auction coordinated by Millicent Parks with items worth tens of thousands of dollars."

"So if you didn't come up here to welcome me home," he said, "or tell me about the babies, why *are* you here?" And while he was asking the questions, "And how did you get in?"

"I knocked. When you didn't answer I," she held up a key, "used this." At Ian's grimace she added, "I have a key to Justin's condo and he has a key to mine. For emergencies."

"So what's your emergency?" he asked.

"The storm uprooted that massive oak by the parking lot which is now resting on top of nine cars, one of them the vehicle I was supposed to drive back to the crisis center this morning to pick up *my* car which, as it turns out, is sitting in two feet of water in *their* parking lot thanks to the Bronx River spilling over its banks at some point in the night. Streets are flooded, trees and power lines are down all over the county and there's a state of emergency in effect so taxis aren't running. I came up to ask Justin for a ride to work."

"Do you hear yourself? There's a state of emergency. The roads aren't safe. Yet here you are ready to forgo the warnings so you can traipse around town."

"For the record, I never traipse. And please spare me the lecture. I have two patients I must see as soon as possible, others depending on me for treatments due today, and some I'd like to check on to see how they made it through the storm." She turned toward the hallway leading to Justin's bedroom.

"He's not here," Ian said. "Mandatory overtime because of the weather." Which gave Ian the perfect opportunity to play hero. "Give me a minute to get changed, and I'll drive you wherever you need to go."

"I don't need you to—"

"Yes you do, sweetheart."

Luckily, Jaci's cellphone rang because she looked to be gearing up for one major league verbal smack down. She checked the number and answered. "Hi, Mrs. Lewis. Yes. Don't worry. I said I'd be there and I will." She listened. "If I have to walk a little that's no problem. Uh huh. See you soon."

She ended the call and looked up at Ian. "What are you waiting for? I need to get on the road. Meet me in the parking lot."

"Yes, ma'am." Ian hurried to his room, for the first time in months meeting a new day with a sense of eager anticipation.

CHAPTER THREE

"THIS is unbelievable," Jaci said. An honest to goodness lake rippled where the heavily traveled thoroughfare of Westchester Avenue should be. After two failed attempts to find a passable road to get to her office to pick up her work car, each wasting valuable time, Jaci had agreed to let Ian drive her around today. And boy was she glad she had.

At the orange barrels blocking entry, Ian turned around. Again.

The annoying GPS voice said, "Recalculating route." Again.

Jaci started to wonder if she would, in fact, be able to keep her promise to Mrs. Lewis.

"I have an idea," Ian said, pulling onto a side road. The man was completely unflappable. While she stared at the horror of murky brown water raging along swollen riverbeds and flowing down roadways into shops and homes, he kept focused on the street ahead of him, steering around downed tree limbs, debris, and standing water, avoiding hanging power lines—some still twisting and sparking.

He sounded official when interacting with law enforcement and emergency personnel who routinely stopped them and cautioned against being out on the roads. A few words from Ian and they were offering directions and detours.

Jaci's phone rang. She looked at the screen. Mrs. Lewis. "Hi, Mrs. Lewis. It's taking a little longer than I expected—"

A male voice interrupted. "This is Barry, Laney's husband. She's frantic. The doctor told her to take her insulin around the same time each morning. She was due at seven and it's almost seven-thirty. She says she feels her heart racing."

"Tell her we're very close. Maybe five minutes. Ten tops." But who knew what they'd find around the next corner.

"Problem?" Ian asked when she ended the call.

"The patient is very anxious about her new diagnosis." Gestational diabetes, on top of being an already nervous, first-time pregnant, soon-to-be new mom.

The car accelerated.

"Thank you for offering to drive me," Jaci said. "This is much worse than I'd imagined."

Ian cut through a grocery store parking lot. "This is nothing. In Iraq there were sand storms and mud storms that made driving next to impossible."

"A mud storm? I've never heard of such a thing."

"It's when it starts to rain during a sand storm. Clumps of mud fall from the sky." He swerved to avoid a plastic garbage can blowing in their direction. "I'd rather deal with the remnants of a weakening hurricane than the IEDs and RPGs intent on killing me," he mumbled.

She'd read about IEDs—improvised explosive devices—and RPGs—rocket propelled grenades—and the threat they posed to the armed forces.

"I think we're here." Ian made a left turn and shot

his arm over to hold her in her seat as he slammed on the brakes to avoid a front-end collision with a huge tree that blocked the road. About ten feet beyond it lay a huge pool of dark water that completely obscured what, according to the sign on the corner, was supposed to be Ashley Court. Luckily the houses were up on small hills so only the bottom portions of the driveways were affected.

"Good thing I wore my rain boots," Jaci said, pulling up her hood and opening her door.

Ian put the Jeep in park and asked, "Where're we headed?"

"*I'm* going to house number thirty-seven, which if the description I was given is correct, is that yellow colonial with blue shutters just before the cul-de-sac." She pointed. "The one with the American flag on the mailbox. *You're* going to wait for me right here."

As Jaci reached in the backseat to retrieve her nursing bag, Ian turned off the car and climbed out which gave him a perfect view of her expression when she lifted the heavy bag with her right hand and received a very sharp, very painful reminder of the large bruise on her upper arm.

He rounded the front fender. "Let me carry that."

"I've got it." Jaci slid the straps onto her left shoulder and the bag connected with her sore ribs. She sucked in a breath, her discomfort a reminder, reinforcing her commitment to help women out of abusive relationships because no one should suffer pain at the hands of another. Ever.

Ian lifted the bag and eased it down her arm, his touch gentle, his eyes concerned. "You okay?"

"What I'm feeling is nothing compared to what I'm

sure Merlene is feeling this morning." And thousands of other women.

Ian closed the door and held out his hand. "Come on. We don't have time to argue. Your patient is waiting."

"You can't come with me." As if she hadn't spoken, he took her hand and guided her up a lawn and around the large root ball of the tree that'd fallen. "Patient privacy. Patient confidentiality." The grass bubbled and squished under her feet. "And your leg." She'd been too angry to care about his limp last night. But this morning... What'd happened to him?

Ian gripped her hand and walked faster, pulling her along, his expression fierce. Determined. "Okay, then." Apparently he felt quite strong about accompanying her. "But only to the driveway."

About halfway to their destination, a tall blond-haired man ran toward them. "Are you Jaci?" he yelled over the wind.

"Mr. Lewis?" she called back, holding on to her hood.

"You have to hurry. Laney's chest feels tight and she can't catch her breath."

Jaci started to run. A sure-footed Ian took the lead, holding tightly to her hand.

"What if she needs to go to the hospital?" Mr. Lewis asked, keeping up beside them. "We're surrounded by water. How the hell am I supposed to get her there?"

"If she needs to go to the hospital, we'll transport her," Jaci said, confident because Ian was there to help. They reached the driveway and ran up it. "But I'm hoping it's an anxiety reaction, and once we calm her down she'll be okay."

Mr. Lewis opened the front door and Jaci entered

into a small, dark foyer. "I'm here, Mrs. Lewis." She took the bag from Ian, who remained on the porch.

"Please. Come inside," Mr. Lewis said to Ian.

"I'm fine out here," Ian said. "Go take care of your wife."

Jaci removed her boots and coat.

"Don't be ridiculous," Mr. Lewis said. "I'm not going to leave you standing in the rain. If not for you, Jaci wouldn't have made it out here."

Ian laughed. "You don't know her," he said. "She'd have found a way."

He'd grown to know her so well in such a short period of time. But rather than comment, Jaci left the men and approached her new patient, a dark-haired beauty in obvious distress, sitting at the edge of the couch, her fist clutched to her chest. Despite her rapid, deep, gasping breaths, her color—though pale—was without any signs of cyanosis.

"Hi, Mrs. Lewis." She went down on her knees to look her patient in the eye. "I'm Jaci, your nurse." She took the woman's cold, clammy free hand in hers. "First thing we need to do is get your breathing under control."

Jaci called over her shoulder to Mr. Lewis, "Do you have a small paper bag?" then turned back to her patient. "Look into my eyes and breathe with me. In." She demonstrated. "Out."

Cabinets slammed in the kitchen. "Where do we keep the lunch bags?" Mr. Lewis called out in frustration. "I can't see a thing in here."

Ian knelt down beside Jaci, completely calm. "No electricity." He held out a paper pharmacy bag. "I saw this on the dining room table."

"Perfect. Thank you," she said to Ian. Then, "Breathe into the bag," she said to Mrs. Lewis, positioning it over her nose and mouth. "You can hold it," she suggested, to give her patient something to do.

Now to distract her. "This is my friend, Ian," Jaci said. "He's volunteered to be my chauffeur for the day."

Mrs. Lewis nodded. The bag puffed and crumpled. Her respirations started to decrease.

Ian smiled.

Boy how Jaci had missed those mischievous, playful dimples.

A glass broke in the kitchen. Mr. Lewis cursed.

"Nice to meet you, ma'am," Ian said then stood. "I'd better go check on your husband."

Although Jaci couldn't see Mrs. Lewis's mouth, her eyes crinkled a bit like maybe she'd smiled, too.

"Do you know if you're having a boy or a girl?" Jaci asked to make conversation.

Mrs. Lewis shook her head then removed the bag from her mouth. "We want it…to be a surprise."

"I think when I get pregnant I'd like the sex of my baby to be a surprise, too," Jaci said. "My sister has four-week-old twin girls. They are absolutely adorable."

Mrs. Lewis set the bag in her lap, her breathing almost normal. "Twins? I'm petrified at the thought of one baby." She looked down lovingly and caressed her large, pregnant belly.

"Have you considered taking a parenting class at the hospital?" Jaci reached into her nursing carryall to take out her computer, blood pressure cuff, and stethoscope. "I hear they're wonderful for first timers. Graduates of the program bring in their infants so you can hold them." She retrieved her baggie of business cards. "You get to observe them changing diapers and clothes. Then you practice on realistic dolls. Maybe it'd help put your mind at ease."

"I think I'd like that," Mrs. Lewis said, raising a hand to push a swag of hair behind her ear.

Jaci found the rubber-banded bundle she sought, pulled off the top card and held it out. "This has the contact information for the woman who runs programing at the hospital. There's also a website you can visit."

Mrs. Lewis took the card. "Thank you."

"You feeling a little better now, Mrs. Lewis?" Jaci asked.

"It's Laney. And yes." She inhaled a deep breath and let it out. "I'm feeling better now that you're here."

"Any pain?"

"No."

"I'm sure they're going to be elevated, but I want to get a quick set of vitals then we'll do your insulin and get you breakfast while I do my documentation." She'd check the vitals again before leaving. While applying the blood pressure cuff, Jaci asked, "Do you have any allergies?"

Laney shook her head.

Jaci pumped up the cuff. "And you've self-administered two doses of insulin at your doctor's office with no problems?"

Laney nodded. "But there was a nurse with me. And the doctor was just down the hall in case anything went wrong."

Jaci entered the BP result in the computer without making a big deal about the fact it was significantly elevated. "Well today I'm here with you so no worries." She checked Laney's pulse—elevated—and respiratory rate—within normal limits. "Now to check your blood sugar."

"I have my glucometer and insulin pen set up on the dining room table."

"Shall we?" Jaci held out a hand to help Laney up.

As if conjured out of thin air, Mr. Lewis appeared. "Sometimes she gets dizzy when she stands up." He took over the task of assisting Laney. Jaci looked on as husband and wife shared a look so loving, a touch so tender and caring, that the specialness of their relationship made her momentarily envious. So she took the opportunity to assess the living environment. A comfortable-sized living room—carpeted—opening into a small eat-in kitchen with a tiled floor. Everything was clean and neat with no visible safety hazards noted.

And no Ian. "Where's Ian?" she asked.

"Out back lighting the barbeque grill. We're going to make you ladies a nice hearty breakfast. Scrambled eggs with cheese, whole wheat toast, and the hot beverage of your choice." He smiled. "As long as tea, coffee, or hot chocolate is one of your choices."

Jaci was about to say they couldn't possibly stay for breakfast because it was totally inappropriate and unprofessional and she had to get to her next patient, when Ian strolled into the room. "Now don't go getting me into trouble, Barry."

That was Ian. In a room with someone for five minutes and he'd made a friend.

"I told you," he went on. "Jaci's in charge. It's her call. I'm just the hired help."

Hired help? Jaci glanced at him through narrowed eyes. Exactly what type of compensation was he expecting?

Ian winked and Jaci's insides fluttered. She was in big trouble.

"It's the least we can do to say thank you for coming out in this terrible weather," Mr. Lewis said.

Ian raised his eyebrows, tilted his head and nodded from behind Mr. Lewis, a nonverbal 'he has a point.'

"The electric company doesn't expect power to be restored in our area for at least two days," Laney offered. "If we don't eat the food in our fridge it will spoil."

"A dozen eggs." Ian tsk tsked. "Laid in vain. Wasted. Because we didn't eat them."

"And you *did* rush Ian out with no breakfast," Mr. Lewis said.

Ian jumped in with, "My stomach growled." He held up both hands. "I wasn't complaining. I'm happy to be here." He turned away and mumbled, "Even if I am about to keel over."

"Please say you'll stay," Laney said, placing her now warm hand on Jaci's forearm, looking more relaxed.

Oy. Three against one. "Okay," she relented. "But I need you both with me for the next fifteen minutes," so she could observe Laney's blood sugar monitoring and insulin injection techniques and offer instruction/ encouragement where needed, as well as review diet, the signs and symptoms of hypoglycemia and how to handle a hypoglycemic episode.

"I've got the pan heating," Ian said, looking at his watch. "Breakfast will be served promptly at zero-eight-hundred."

"You'd have made a good soldier," Ian said as Jaci programmed the address of their next stop into the GPS. "I'd have welcomed you on my team in a heartbeat." She worked hard, didn't complain, and remained calm in a crisis.

"Green's not my color," Jaci joked.

She'd look good wrapped in burlap. "Honestly. You were great back there."

A blush tinted her cheeks. "Just doing my job."

And in the process, she'd given him even more things to like about her. Professionalism. Compassion. Competence. Confidence. All very sexy qualities in a woman.

He veered as far to the right as safely possible to drive through the shallowest edge of a length of standing water.

"You're an okay cook," Jaci said.

"Breakfast is my specialty. I'm happy to make it for you any day of the week." Preferably after a night of hot sex.

"I know what you're thinking. Stop it."

"Okay, smarty pants." He glanced over at her. "What was I thinking?"

"That you'd like to cook me breakfast after a night of sex."

Technically he'd specified 'hot' sex, but okay, he'd give it to her.

She smiled and nodded. "I was right, wasn't I?"

Damn her smile did things to him. And her teasing tone. If Ian wasn't mistaken, the light, fluttery feeling in his gut might just be happiness. "Considering I haven't been up close and personal with a naked female body since you and I were together," the GPS interrupted and told him to prepare for a right turn, "lots of things get me thinking about sex. So don't go getting all cocky that you know me so well." But she did, and it hadn't taken her long to figure him out, which, in addition to the distraction of attraction, was another reason he needed to keep his distance. So she didn't pick up on his PTSD crap. Thinking him weak, pathetic and unstable was unacceptable. It shouldn't matter, but it did.

"So you haven't been with…?"

"No," he said. He'd been at war for nine months, in the hospital for three. When exactly...?

"I haven't, either," she said quietly.

No declaration had ever made him happier. Ian junior started to swell with delight. "You know, maybe we could change the subject." He shifted in his seat and adjusted his pants. "Because I'm about ten seconds from pulling off the road, hauling you into the backseat, and initiating a few let's-you-and-me-get-reacquainted activities."

Eyes wide, Jaci said, "You wouldn't dare."

That sounded like a challenge.

"Oh yes I would." If she wasn't working and didn't have to get to her next visit. Just to have a little fun he swerved. She screamed. "You're crazy."

Yup. Certifiable.

After leaving her fourth visit in the city of Yonkers, Jaci looked at her watch and said, "Turn left here. I'll treat you to lunch."

A quick scan of the neighborhood and Ian had no intention of letting her out of the car.

"Turn right." Jaci directed him into the parking lot of what looked like an abandoned, brick building that could have once been a high or middle school. "Drive around back."

"What is this place?" Ian asked, pulling into a spot next to a rusted out frame of a car with cinder blocks where the tires should be. Dozens of down-on-their-luck types milled around a long cement sidewalk. Loose fitting clothes. Bags. Strollers. Hundreds of places to stash a weapon.

Lately Ian was not a fan of crowds.

"The local soup kitchen," Jaci said. "Come on." She opened the door and climbed out before he could stop her. Did the woman have no concern for her well-being at all?

"Jaci, I don't think—"

A huge black man wearing an oversized football jersey that stretched tight across his rounded chest and belly approached her.

Ian hurried to Jaci's side, wishing he'd thought to strap on a firearm before leaving the condo.

"Hey there, Big D," Jaci said with a wave. "You checking in on your grandma like I told you?"

Ian let out a relieved breath, but remained on guard as all eyes turned in their direction.

"Sure am," the big man said.

"She taking all her meds?"

"I'm pouring them every Sunday like you taught me."

"She's lucky to have you."

Big D smiled proudly.

"Give her my regards, will you?"

"Sure will."

On their way into the building, several other people standing on a long line said their hellos. Jaci, looking totally at ease in her surroundings, offered a warm, familiar greeting to each of them.

Ian stood tall, focused on not limping, and assessed everyone he passed for a possible threat.

When they reached a large industrial-sized kitchen an older woman wearing a smudged white chef's apron and a hairnet called out, "Jaci, honey. You are a gift from the gods."

Jaci hugged the woman. "Where is everyone?"

"Not one volunteer showed up." She talked while she worked, efficiently slathering peanut butter on pieces of white bread. "Russell has no electric and a foot of water in his basement. School was cancelled and Angie has no one to watch her kids. So it's me, Red and Cooper."

With what looked like more than a hundred people lined up for lunch. They were significantly outnumbered with him unarmed. Ian fought the urge to grab Jaci and escape out the back door of the kitchen. He was home in New York, he reminded himself, trying to calm his rising tension. The people outside weren't hostiles. He doubted any foreign operatives mingled among them. They were simply hungry people looking for a meal.

Or so it seemed. And a friendly gathering could turn into an angry, violent mob in an instant. Yelling. Pushing and shoving. A distraction. Gunfire. Two men hit. A bomb blast. He stared at the one double-door entry into the large room, waiting for trouble, starting to sweat.

Get it together, Ice.

A warm hand on his upper arm brought him back to his senses. "Mary, this is my friend, Ian."

He reached out a clammy hand to Mary, relieved when she held up her plastic-gloved hands instead of shaking it.

"Put us to work," he said, assuming that's why they were there, knowing the sooner they got everyone fed, the sooner they could leave this place.

"We have no gas to cook," Mary said. "Water's questionable, but the fridge is working. We're doing peanut butter and jelly sandwiches, sliced apples, cake and chocolate milk."

"Apples?" Jaci asked.

"I know," Mary said. "Half the people who come don't have sturdy enough teeth to bite into an apple. But a local farm dropped off a couple of bushels. We'd planned to make a cobbler but without working ovens

Red and Cooper are peeling, coring, and slicing them, then soaking the wedges in orange juice. That'll have to do."

Jaci walked over to a small box on a wire shelving unit, took out a hairclip, and put her hair up in a ponytail. "Gloves are over there." She pointed to a box to her right. "Paper plates beside them. Knives are by the stove. If you'll portion out the cake stacked on that table," she motioned to the left with her head, "I'll get the tables, utensils and trays ready."

Ian spent the next ten minutes cutting up an assortment of day-old bakery items, placing them on small paper plates, which went on large metal trays that got inserted into a rolling food service rack. All the while he watched Jaci move around the room with purpose, lining the long rows of tables with plastic sheeting, stacking trays on the end of the serving line, and wrapping plastic forks in napkins. She knew exactly what needed to be done and did it, like she'd worked there many times before.

There was much he didn't know about socialite Jaci Piermont.

Mary came to stand beside him. "She's something, isn't she?"

"Yeah." Something special.

"Been coming here since she was a little girl, first with a group from her church, then with her mother and sister." Mary put two bottles of liquid chocolate on the counter. "Would you get me four gallons of milk from the fridge? Make sure you check the dates."

Ian did as requested and they poured the milk into a large tub, added the chocolate, and Mary stirred the mixture with a long paddle. "After her mom's accident, we didn't see Jaci around much. But since she's been back working in the area we see her at least once a week. Depending on her schedule, she either helps out with lunch or just stops by to drop off food donations."

Did Mary know who Jaci was? A member of the powerful Piermont family? From what Justin had told him, a girl who'd grown up with a butler and chauffeurs on the largest estate in one of the richest towns in the U.S.?

As if she could read his mind, Mary said, "Yeah. I know. Only because years ago I recognized her mother. Jaci doesn't talk about it, so neither do I. To the people in the area, she's a hard-working, generous, well-liked community health nurse."

She sure didn't look like a socialite with her functional black slacks tucked into black, red and white plaid rain boots, a plain white blouse, only a hint of makeup, and no jewelry other than a discount-store wristwatch. Her perfectly manicured, brightly painted fingernails were the only tell that she was accustomed to the finer things in life.

"It's one o'clock," Jaci said. "We ready to serve?"

In a flurry of activity plastic cups appeared before him and Ian dunked a pitcher into the tub of chocolate milk to fill them. A tall, muscular man with red hair rolled out a rack containing trays of sliced apples in small plastic dishes. A short, dark-haired man pushed over a rack containing trays of Mary's sandwiches. In a few short minutes they were lined up with Mary on trays, paper plates, utensils, and sandwiches, Jaci on bottled water and coffee, Ian on milk, Red on apples, and Cooper on cakes.

"Let 'em in," Cooper called out. Within seconds the large cafeteria filled with people. Some hurried to claim a seat. Others headed straight for the line forming for food.

The volume of voices swelled. The room seemed to shrink in size. The air heated. Thickened. A colorful sea of unfamiliar faces, old and weathered, young and disheartened, dirty and scarred, floated before him. Afro-American. Caucasian. Latino. Central American.

An olive skinned man who averted his eyes. Why? What had he done?

Ian froze with his hand mid-way to placing a cup of milk on the man's tray.

"He's only here for lunch," Red said, carefully taking the cup from Ian's hand and serving it. "How long you been back?" he asked.

Ian cleared his throat. "Military hospital three months. Home three weeks."

Jaci dropped a mug which bounced on the rubber drainage mats under their feet.

Damn. Had she heard? He didn't dare look at her.

"Iraq?"

"Yeah."

"It'll get better," Red said.

What the hell did he know?

Red raised the short sleeve of his drab grey T-shirt to reveal a Semper Fi tat. "I had a rough time re-acclimating, too. Took about a year, but I managed to get it together. So will you."

Yeah. Red had gotten it together enough to show up for his minimum wage job at the soup kitchen looking like he'd just rolled out of bed after a long night of hard partying. If that worked for him, fine.

But Ian wanted more. Needed a good, high paying job. And soon.

Ten years in the Army and successful completion

of Ranger School, in his opinion, the toughest most intense training program in all branches of the military, had to be worth something.

CHAPTER FOUR

AFTER a thankfully quiet trip from the soup kitchen, during which Jaci sat uncharacteristically still and quiet, Ian pulled up to visit number five right on schedule. In this more suburban part of the county, they didn't pass any visible flooding, but there was plenty of damage from high winds.

"I'll be out as soon as I can," Jaci said when she opened the rear door to get her nursing bag.

"Take your time." Ian reclined the seat and closed his eyes, although he wouldn't admit it, happy to relax for a few minutes.

Maybe he'd dozed off. More likely he'd been lost in thought when a knock on his window made him jump so high he banged his left thigh on the steering wheel hard enough to send black dots floating through his vision.

At Jaci's look of concern, Ian swallowed down the slew of curses demanding to be set free and resisted the urge to punch something. Instead he tried out some of the anger management techniques his rehab therapist had taught him. He inhaled. Exhaled. Counted back from ten. Made it to six. Swallowing down a string of curses he reached to turn the key in the ignition with his right hand and hit the switch to lower the electric window with his left. "Sorry. I must have fallen asleep."

"I didn't mean to scare you," Jaci said. "Your leg." She leaned into the car and looked down at it. "Are you all right?"

"You didn't scare me. You startled me. There's a difference." He leaned forward, positioning his head directly in front of hers, crowding her so she'd move out of his space. Worked like a charm. "My leg is fine."

She didn't look convinced.

"Why are you out here with me instead of inside with your patient?"

"I'll, uh, work it out." She turned back to the house. "You rest."

So she *had* overheard his conversation with Red. "Get back here," Ian yelled through the window as it closed. Good thing she'd stopped, because when he climbed out of his Jeep it took a few moments of gradual weight-bearing on his left leg before he felt confident enough to walk on it. "I don't need to rest." Or be babied or pitied or treated like he was weak. Useless. "Keep me busy. Give me something to do."

"The Janoviches have no electricity. The house is cool and Mrs. Janovich can't tolerate anything more than a sheet on her lower extremities. We want to move her hospital bed closer to the fireplace."

"They put the blasted thing together inside the room," an elderly, slightly hunched man wearing a green cardigan said as he walked onto the porch. "Never thought I'd have reason to move it."

"We'll get it done, sir," Ian said.

"Mr. Janovich, this is my friend, Ian."

"Good man driving our Jaci around on a day like today." Mr. Janovich held out his hand and Ian shook it. "Nice to meet you."

Our Jaci. Damn if Ian wasn't starting to feel possessive of her, too.

The main living area of the house was rundown and cluttered. Neglected. Jaci led him down a long, dark hallway, turning to stop him prior to entering the room at its end. "Give me a minute."

"Mrs. Janovich," she said quietly as she walked into the room. "My friend is right outside. Is it alright with you if he comes in so we can figure out the best way to move this bed?"

He didn't hear a response but Jaci added, "Nakisha and I are going to pull up the sheet." The woman groaned her displeasure.

Mr. Janovich arrived at his side. "That complex regional pain syndrome, especially the allodynia, is nasty business." He handed Ian a screwdriver. "I think if we remove the door from the hinges we'll have a little more room."

"Come in," Jaci whispered from the doorway. "Try to be quiet. Today is not a good day."

It took under five seconds for Ian to come to the conclusion there was no way to get that hospital bed out of the tiny room with the patient in it. He looked at Jaci who stood on one side of the bed and a heavy, dark-skinned woman in navy blue scrubs who stood on the other. "Can she sit in a chair for a few minutes?"

The two women both looked down at their patient who, with her pale, sunken cheeks, furrowed brow, and tissue-paper-thin, wrinkled skin, looked years older than her husband. Constant pain aged a person. Some days Ian felt closer to sixty than thirty.

"There's no need for that," Mr. Janovich said. "I'm sure we can—"

"Ian's right," Jaci said. "We've been avoiding the inevitable. Even if we did manage to get the bed through the door, all the jostling would probably cause more pain than a quick transfer to her wheelchair."

"Let me stay here," the patient begged. "I'm fine right here."

"Your lower extremities are chilled and your feet are like ice," Jaci said. "Nakisha and I will help you." She motioned for the nurse's aide to get the wheelchair which sat collapsed against a wall in the corner of the room. "We'll go slow. There's no rush." Jaci kept her voice calm, soothing.

Ian wished he'd had a nurse like her during his long recovery.

Jaci looked over at him. "If you and Mr. Janovich could make a space for the bed in the family room, that'd be great," Jaci said.

While he helped tie up about one hundred pounds of old newspapers and magazines in easy to lift bundles for recycling, Ian listened to the sounds coming from the end of the hallway. Screams. Crying. Jaci's calm reassurance and gentle coaxing. How did she do it? How did she deal with anguish, pain and poverty day in and day out and still maintain her positive outlook and sense of humor?

He'd known she worked as a nurse. She never spoke much about it, and for some reason he'd pictured her gallivanting from ritzy estate to ritzy estate checking on post op liposuctions and face lifts, maybe the occasional Botox injection gone wrong. Prior to today, he'd never pictured Jaci serving meals in a soup kitchen or tending to a woman in a filthy, smelly, water-damaged basement apartment while her alcoholic husband lay passed out on the couch—which he knew because he'd flat out refused to let her enter the dilapidated building alone. He'd never imagined what she actually did in the course of a day. The people she helped, the lives she impacted.

His respect for her quadrupled.

By six o'clock that night Jaci had completed eight patient visits while Ian had wet-vacuumed three basements, fixed a sump pump, hooked up two generators, hauled wood, chopped wood, drove to find an open convenience store for water, batteries, and/or non-perishable food, got two propane tanks filled, worked with three men to move the metal roof that'd blown off a shed, and rescued a cat from on top of a refrigerator in a basement flooded with over a foot of water. His left leg throbbed, his body ached, and if he closed his eyes he'd be asleep in under a minute.

He hadn't felt this good in months.

In an upsetting turn of events, Jaci slowed her stride so Ian could keep up with her as they walked from his Jeep to the entrance of their complex. During the course of their long, exhausting day his left-sided limp had progressed from slight to pronounced. Yet each time she'd suggested he rest, he'd refused, making himself available to assist her patients and their families and in two instances, neighbors. "When you get inside you should take two ibuprofen and a hot bath."

"Care to join me?" he wiggled his eyebrows.

She landed a playful punch to his upper arm. Just like old times. Except things between them had changed. Because Jaci had dared to question the fun, carefree, no commitment nature of their relationship. Because she'd dared to think she didn't have to forgo the money in her trust because the idea of marriage, of someone monitoring her every move and commenting on/trying to control her every activity left her cold. That maybe her obligatory five years living as wife to a husband—at five million dollars per year—could actually be spent with a man she liked and found attractive, a man who had seemed to like her, too, a man who didn't crowd her and who spent more time overseas than at home. The ideal solution!

But fearing rejection and the ruination of a friendship she'd valued, Jaci had put off the all-important discussion. And, with the clock ticking on Ian's departure, she'd made a poorly thought out impulsive move meant to entice him and show him just how good the two of them together could be. She'd given him exactly what he'd been angling for since they'd met—her body.

And once he'd gotten what he'd wanted from her, he'd walked away—ran actually. Without a backward glance. Making the hours she'd spent in his arms, feeling wanted, cared for and hopeful, that much more heartbreaking.

Valuable lesson learned: Never let your guard down.

So where did that leave them? After everything that'd happened in the past year, could they still be friends? Did he even want that? "I get why you didn't write me or e-mail me while you were in Iraq. But after you were injured, when you were back in the states recovering in the hospital, why didn't you call me then? I'm a nurse. Maybe there's something I could have done to help in your recovery." Then it occurred to her. "Unless you already had someone with you."

"I didn't."

"So you'd rather—"

"I'm sorry if I was too busy fighting off the surgeons who wanted to amputate my leg, fighting infection, and fighting my own damn demons to pick up the phone for a chat," he snapped in what used to be an atypical show of anger.

It must have been terrible. "I would have come to you," she said, swiping her ID in the security scanner. Despite everything, she would not have left him to suffer alone.

"Which is why I didn't call," he said quietly as he opened the door and waited for her to walk through.

She stopped to look up at him.

"Listen." He took her by the arm and led her into the lobby. "It was my decision to join the army. To serve and protect my country. I knew the risks, and I accepted them. Why should I inconvenience you because of my life choices?"

"It wouldn't have been an inconvenience." Not really.

"Can we not talk about this right now?" He inclined his head and traced his eyebrows with his thumb and middle fingers. "I think this conversation would turn out better for me after you've had a good night's sleep."

Good call. They entered the elevator and she pressed the buttons for the fourth and fifth floors. "Thank you for coming with me today." Had she been on her own, she no doubt wouldn't have gotten home for hours.

"Thank you for letting me tag along on a day in the secret life of Jaci Piermont."

He'd done a lot more than tag along. "Not as glamorous as you thought, huh?"

"No. It wasn't quite what I'd expected," he admitted, placing her nursing bag on the floor and bracing his right shoulder on the side wall of the elevator so he could relieve the pressure on his left leg. "I can't help wondering what compels local society's favorite princess to circulate among the sick and elderly and the poor and disenfranchised, in dirty sometimes dangerous conditions, when she has the means to join the ladies-who-lunch-and-plan-fundraisers-to-benefit-the-less-fortunate crowd. And why she kept it a secret from a friend who she would have dropped everything for, to take care of him in the hospital."

"Mom didn't come from money," Jaci explained. "She always said, 'If you want to make a difference in people's lives you need to be an active participant in those lives.' She felt strongly that simply taking the easy way out and throwing money at a problem didn't make it go away. And I agree." As far as not telling people every detail of how she filled her time, it was no one's business. Working as a nurse and with the Woman's Crisis Center gave her a sense of purpose, of accomplishment and fulfillment. Why taint that by telling people who would only respond similarly to how Ian had. 'Why work when you don't have to?' 'Don't go into that building, don't go down to that part of town, it's not safe.' Just because an area was rundown and inhabited by poor people, didn't mean it was unsafe. Residents of the low income housing projects she frequented looked out for her, and if she needed to, she coordinated visits with another nurse or requested a police escort.

But by far, the biggest reason she didn't share her occupation as a nurse and exactly what she did for the crisis center—at least in addition to her fundraising responsibilities—was if word got round to Jerry Three he'd make it impossible for her to do the 'demeaning' work she loved. He'd agreed to let Jaci and Jena attend college for nursing purely to keep them out of his hair and so they could help with their mother's care. But in his opinion women of high society were nothing more than bejeweled pets meant to adorn a man's arm and cater to his every whim. And his stepsisters were nothing more than instruments for advantageous pairing with his business associates to inflate his bottom line.

Not gonna happen. No matter how hard he pushed. She and Jena both deserved more than men only interested in their money or business dealings with their father's company.

The doors opened on the fourth floor. Jaci turned to take her nursing bag, but Ian had already picked it up and was exiting the elevator.

"Ian, please. You shouldn't walk any more than you have to. You need to res—"

"If you tell me to rest one more time I'm going to kiss you so long and so deep that resting will be the last thing you'll want me to do."

That sounded sooo good. She smiled. "You really should…." 'Rest' did a daring shimmy-shake on the tip of her tongue.

Ian picked her up by the waist and set her back to the wall. Their eyes level, the width of a paperclip separating their lips. "Say it," he whispered, his breath warm its scent enticing. "I dare you."

Seconds from wrapping her arms and legs around him, and blurting out, "rest," Jaci was saved from an embarrassing show of need by a neighbor carrying his trash down the opposite end of the hallway.

Ian set her down but kept his eyes locked with hers. "The day I am physically incapable of accompanying a woman to her door is the day I'd rather be dead than alive."

Behind the door in question two babies with exceptional lung capacity cried out their displeasure for everyone in the complex to hear. Jaci set her forehead to the cool metal. After a night of disrupted sleep, during which she'd gotten up each time Jena had, followed by a full day of work made more demanding in the aftermath of a hurricane turned tropical storm, she'd give anything for a nap.

Ian took her by the hand. It felt so good. Big, warm, and strong. "Come upstairs." He gave a little tug. "Decompress for a few minutes." He understood.

"I can't." But she allowed herself to be led back to the elevator. "I should be jumping into the fray to help Jena."

"In an hour you'll be recharged and in better shape than you are now."

Maybe. She fished her phone out of her coat pocket and hit two on speed dial. "Hey, it's me," she said when Jena answered. Dual unhappy babies raged in the background. "I'm just checking in. Everything okay?" Of course things weren't okay. Jena was alone with two very loud, screaming infants. She needed help. She needed her sister. Jaci stopped.

"We're good." Jena sounded way more cheerful than Jaci'd expected.

"Right," Jaci said, heading back to the condo. Tired or not, Jena and the babies had to come first.

"No. Really. Hold on." After a muffled, "Would you hand me that cloth?" Jena resumed talking to Jaci. "When one cries it gets the other one started. Just like mom said we did."

"Is someone there with you?"

"Yes. Mrs. Calvin. And she's just as wonderful as you said."

Jaci let out a relieved breath. "So you're okay for another hour or two?"

"We're getting ready to do baths, then it's bottles and bedtime. In an hour or two I'll be ready to chat over dinner and an over-sized glass of the Sauvignon Blanc I found in your fridge."

Jaci smiled, looking forward to it. "It's a plan. See you then."

After washing up in the bathroom, foraging through Ian's kitchen for a snack, and washing the dishes in the sink, Jaci called her favorite Italian bistro and ordered four chicken Marsala dinners to be delivered at eight o'clock. Treating Ian to dinner was the least she could do. And Justin would have to come home from the police station at some point.

Finding the pill bottle she sought in the cabinet by the refrigerator Jaci called out to Ian, "Did you take some ibuprofen?"

No answer.

"Ian?"

No answer.

She filled a glass with water and carried it, and the medicine, into the living room where she found Ian still in his jacket, still wearing his boots, still sitting on the sofa where she'd left him…fast asleep. In the hospital for three months, home for three weeks, it was amazing he'd managed to accomplish as much as he had before collapsing from exhaustion.

He looked so handsome, his face completely relaxed, his lips parted, his jet black hair short but thick on top, shaved to his scalp on the sides. So big and strong, but recovering from a serious injury. Her wounded warrior. Well, not hers but. Oh, to heck with it.

Jaci knelt at his feet to remove his wet boots and socks, noticing the edge of a dark red scar looping around his left ankle—which was swollen. Hesitant to get caught snooping where she didn't belong, or worse, thrown to the ground like an enemy soldier, Jaci resisted the urge to push his pant leg up farther.

Instead she put his boots on the mat by the door and went to his bedroom to get a couple of pillows and a comforter to put under his leg to elevate it.

"Ian," she said quietly, hesitant to touch him after what'd happened when she'd tried to wake him that morning. "Lie down."

"Jaci?" he asked sleepily. "Sorry. I need a few…"

Since he recognized her she placed her palm on his cheek to guide him. "I brought you a pillow." With a gentle push, he slid to the side and lowered his head. "Lift your legs." He winced and groaned in pain, more asleep than awake. Jaci helped him lift his left leg onto the couch. "Scoot onto your back." He didn't move. "C'mon, Ian. Help me." She pulled his right hip toward her and he shifted onto his back. A minute later Jaci had the comforter stuffed under his leg, a knit blanket over top of him, and the alarm on her cell phone set for seven forty-five.

With the scent of Ian on the pillow beneath her head, she settled into the other couch.

Jaci jolted awake to a gruff male shout. Her fist pressed to her pounding heart, she scanned her dimly lit surroundings, remembering she was at Ian's condo.

"Answer me." He gave an order.

On the verge of telling him to stop yelling, she caught a glimpse of him in the light from the kitchen, still lying on the sofa across from her, his eyes closed.

"Can't move." He thrashed his head from side to side, strained like trying to escape something, his breathing fast and heavy.

"Ian?"

No response.

Jaci sat up not sure if she should wake him. Perspiration beaded on his forehead.

"Hurts." Ian let out a heart-wrenching groan. He jerked his upper body from side to side. "Dying. Medic."

Jaci got off the sofa and walked toward him. "You're home in New York," she said, trying to reorient him to the present.

"No. Can't leave my men," he mumbled.

She stepped closer. "Ian. Wake up. It's Jaci."

"Jaci," he whispered on exhalation like the name soothed him.

"Yes." She walked to beside the sofa and kneeled.

"Jaci," she said. His body relaxed.

"You're home. You're safe."

"Not safe." He stiffened and resumed the fight against invisible restraints. The knit blanket tightened around his midsection. "They're out there."

Her heart squeezed. What had he gone through? How could she help him?

"Dead," he mumbled, grief-stricken. "All dead."

At his devastated tone Jaci knew she had no choice but to wake him, to rescue him from the horror of his nightmare. That morning he'd awoken oriented and aroused as soon as he'd recognized it was her body pinned beneath him. Maybe she could expedite recognition and avoid a full body slam to the thankfully plush area rug by going in for a kiss instead.

Deciding it was worth a try, she stood, leaned in, and careful not to touch any other part of him, set her lips to his.

Within seconds he was kissing her back. Yes! Tentative turned wow turned big time mistake when his hand clutched the back of her head, applied way more pressure than necessary, and mashed her lips onto his. Triumph morphed into concern when his strong arm clamped around her upper body, dragged her on top of him, and squeezed her chest to his in what she hoped was an uncomfortably tight, one-armed hug and not some military maneuver meant to kill by restricting an adversary's ability to draw air into the lungs.

"Please don't be a dream," he murmured against her lips. Pleading. "Please don't be a dream. I need you to be real," he said. Desperate. Clinging to her like he'd plummet into an abyss if he let go.

"I'm real, Ian. And you're—"

"Thank you. Thank you, God." He moved her head, buried his face in the side of her neck and inhaled deeply. "I remember…every detail of our night together. I have recreated it in my mind hundreds of times," he said, his mouth moving along her skin, his hands sliding under the back of her sweater set. "Your smooth skin. Your sweet scent. And your taste," he opened his mouth and took a toothless bite that ended in a wet, devouring, vision-blurring kiss on her neck. "Succulent."

She lifted her head to look at him. "Are you still talking in your sleep or did you honestly just compare me to a perfectly cooked pork chop?"

He smiled. "Succulent as in ripe, flavorful, and desirable."

Man he had a way with words. "Welcome back."

He turned his head, giving her a good view of his ear. "Was it a bad one?"

"Yeah. You want to talk about it?" she asked.

"No." He rocked his pelvis, as if she hadn't already noticed his erection against her thigh. "I'd rather replace a bad memory with a good one."

If only it were that easy. She moved her thumb over

a small scar on his right temple and one on his chin that she hadn't noticed before. "You find that's an effective way of dealing with your nightmares?"

He looked back up at her. Serious. Sincere. "I sure would like to find out."

"With me?" She rubbed her index finger along his plump lower lip.

"Only you." He sucked her finger deep into his mouth. Her body responded with an instantaneous surge of arousal while her mind, focusing on his 'only you', responded with an intense yearning for intimacy between them.

"You were in my head for months," he said, easing her head closer to his. "Brightening dreary days, filling the silence, urging extra caution so I could return to you, hold you and make love to you." With both hands on either side of her face he guided her the short distance to his lips and kissed her. "After the blast I got so caught up in grief and pain I lost you. It seems I'm no good on my own anymore. I need you, Jaci." He kissed her again, his ardor growing, his tongue thrusting into her, mimicking the movement of his hips.

Jaci's body came alive for the first time in over a year, reawakened by his touch. And she wanted him just as much as he wanted her.

She shifted her lower body to straddle him, accidentally kicking his left thigh. He stiffened and sucked in a breath. How could she have forgotten? She pushed off his chest and sat up, keeping most of her weight on her knees. "Maybe we shouldn't. Your leg." She started to climb off of him.

He clasped his large hands around her waist to stop her. "My leg is fine. Trust me, the ache that has my full attention is higher and more centrally located."

"You mean here?" she asked innocently and reached back to caress him through his jeans, up along his zipper, down between his legs to his butt.

Ian let out a shaky breath. "Before we get started, I think I'd better apologize in advance for any…uh, misfire."

Restrained laughter tickled the inside of her belly at his unease with the topic. If what he'd said was true, and she had no reason to believe it wasn't, he hadn't been with a woman in over a year. Of course he'd be on the edge. "Bit of a hair trigger?" she teased, continuing to rub him.

"Yeah," he said, in deep concentration. "As much as I despise the thought of the word 'premature' being in any way associated with what we are about to do, before my injury I'd spent at minimum one thousand hours envisioning how we'd celebrate my return home. And right this minute you have me so revved up 'premature' is more a probability than a possibility."

She took pity on him and stopped, intending to slow things down. And have some fun. "In all those 'welcome home' scenarios you've conjured up in that handsome head of yours have any involved role play?"

Interest sparked in his eyes and an I'm-up-for-anything grin formed on his mouth.

Okay then, time to set a little emotional distance. Physical was the name of the game. To stay within the rules of play there would be no feelings involved unless they were directly linked to the pursuit of pleasure. "I am a superior officer," Jaci said. "You will follow my every order and you will address me as ma'am." In the sexy military style she'd heard him use on occasion.

"Yes, ma'am." He lifted his hips, rocked his erection against her yes-right-there-do-not-stop spot and

Jaci realized staying in control of the situation may be a little harder than she'd originally thought. His smile told her he knew exactly what'd just crossed her mind. "To the best of my ability, ma'am."

"Very well," she said, imitating an army officer. "You will remain in control of your…orgasms, Staff Sergeant."

Humor crinkled the skin at the corners of his eyes and a playful smile lightened his expression to the fun, carefree face she remembered from before his most recent trip to Iraq. "Thank you for stating orgasms in the plural, ma'am."

Jaci struggled not to grin so she could issue her next order. "Disrobe from the waist up, soldier." She couldn't wait to see the contours of his broad, muscled chest and big, strong arms.

"I mean no disrespect, ma'am," he answered. "But I will if you will."

Ah what the heck. "Deal."

Since Jaci was sitting up it took all of five seconds for her to yank off her sweater and pull the matching tank over her head. Ian reached up. "Front clasp." He remembered. With a skilled pinch her bra hung open.

"I don't want to know how you got so good at that."

He removed his windbreaker. "I used to steal my sisters' bras from the laundry to practice on them."

Whether true or not, "Good answer." She removed her bra, enjoying all the jostling down below as he worked to remove his T-shirt while lying down.

When he noticed her bare breasts illuminated in the light from the kitchen he stilled. Staring up at them he licked his lips, and Jaci's nipples went hard. "Beautiful," he said with the perfect amount of reverence in his tone as he reached up to cup them…

Just as the door to the condo opened and Justin walked in. At the sight of her he said, "Holy, hell," and slapped his hand over his eyes. "Hi, Jaci." He closed the door.

She flattened herself on Ian's naked chest and he wrapped his arms around her to provide additional cover. "Hi, Justin."

She heard him walk down the hallway toward his bedroom. "It's about time, Ian," he said.

"Shut up, Justin," Ian responded.

"You know you have your own bedroom," Justin said. Adding, "Maybe it's time you started using it," before a door closed.

Jaci looked down the hallway to confirm it was in fact Justin's bedroom door that'd closed and with him behind it, before she started to rise.

Ian stopped her. "Promise me when you stand up you are going to accompany me to my bedroom." Desperation had returned to his voice. "Promise me you are not going to reconsider or change your mind and leave."

"I have no shirt on," Jaci joked. "I'm not leaving so fast."

"Please." He held her tight. Somber.

No way could she leave him when he sounded like he'd die without her, nor did she want to. "The only place I'm going," she slid up the distance needed to kiss his lips, "is to your bed." She shimmied off of him. "Where I hope you will not keep me waiting." She looked at her watch. "I'm having dinner delivered. We have thirty-seven minutes."

CHAPTER FIVE

WHILE Jaci pranced down the hall topless with her clothes clutched to her chest and her blonde curls bouncing, Ian eased his stiff leg to the floor. Thirty-seven minutes. Hell, thirty-seven seconds inside her warm, lush body would likely be enough to finish him off. He stood, waiting for the pins and needles in his leg to subside. He would draw out their time together if he had to channel a lifetime's worth of self-control to do it, because in every single one of his welcome home fantasies, as in real life, her pleasure was as important as his.

He took a tentative step. *Dammit. I am going to have sex. With Jaci. I have been waiting for this moment for over a year. I will not think about the pain in my damn leg. I will not think about the pain in my damn leg.*

"I'm waiting," Jaci called out in flirty invitation. "And I'm naked."

"Do I really have to know that?" Justin yelled through his door.

"Sorry," Jaci said. "I ordered us dinner. It's coming by eight."

If Ian didn't get a move on, dinner would be the only thing coming by eight. Unacceptable. He tried to flex his knee. Couldn't. His muscles had gone into spasm, just like the doctor had warned they might if he over-did it.

"Thanks, Jaci," Justin said.

"Would you two knock off the small talk?" Ian snapped, louder than he'd intended, but he didn't want Jaci getting distracted. By sheer force of will he pow-ered through pain that would typically have sent him back to the couch, until he reached his bedroom. Where he stopped short at the sight of Jaci, the unparalleled Goddess of Lovely, stretched out in full sex kitten on top of his navy blue sheets, in the center of his queen-sized bed. And she was indeed naked. And beautiful, with her creamy white complexion forming a strapless bikini pattern in stark contrast to the enticingly tanned, smooth skin of the rest of her body. Her pink nipples hardened into mini top hats on her rounded breasts, each screaming for attention. His mouth watered.

"Breathe, Staff Sergeant." Jaci smiled her satisfac-tion at his stupor as she wrapped a curl around her finger. "Then close the door, take off your pants, and come hither."

Close door: Check.

Remove pants: Only in the dark. Unfortunate. He gave one last slow, head-to-toe perusal of her stunning body, committing every spectacular inch to memory, hit the light switch and shucked off his jeans and briefs. Check.

Come hither: On his way.

"Hey," Jaci complained. "I want to see you."

Not gonna happen. He could barely stomach how his now deformed leg looked. No way he'd subject Jaci to it. Definite arousal buster.

"Turn the light back on, soldier," she commanded.

"No." He reached into his nightstand for a couple of condoms.

"That is gross insubordination," Jaci said. "I'm in charge."

"I'm going rogue." He half-crawled, half-dragged onto the bed, found her, and covered her soft, heavenly, naked body with his, reveled in the cushion of her breasts and how it felt to be cradled between her thighs. "You feel so good." He kissed her lips, her cheek and neck. Too good. The fierce urge to have her, to thrust into her, over and over, now, with no barrier between them almost got the better of him.

She slid her hands up his back and neck to comb through the hair on the top of his head. "Would you at least still call me ma'am?"

That he could do. "Permission to go down on you, ma'am?"

"Rogue works for me." He heard the smile in her voice. "Permission happily granted, Staff Sergeant." She pulled down his head so she could whisper in his ear. "If you'd like to do a little sightseeing on your journey down under," she forced out a hot breath and tongued his ear, "I wouldn't be adverse to a detour or two."

Yeah. He knew what she wanted and didn't waste a minute getting to it. Trouble was he enjoyed sucking on her breasts as much as she enjoyed having him do it. The feel of her taut, roughened nipple on his tongue had his erection so sensitive even impersonal contact with the mattress served to stimulate him. Her moans, gasps and twitches as he alternated between them, swirling, flicking, squeezing and drawing her into his mouth fast and hard had him moving on before he embarrassed himself.

He left a saliva trail down the center of her ribs,

around her bellybutton, meandering south until his chin grazed her curls. When the scent of her arousal flowed into his nostrils and the finger he'd sent to explore the lips guarding her treasure found her wet and ready for him, things turned urgent. Ian fumbled to locate the condoms he'd left on the bed, ripped open a wrapper, and rolled one on.

The race to the finish was on. Unfortunately he'd taken the lead and needed Jaci to catch up quick. So he settled between her legs, opened her with his thumbs, and set to work.

"My, God, Ian." She clamped her thighs on his head and squirmed her hips. "That is so good. But I need—" He eased his tongue into her opening. "Yes." She spread her legs wide. "More." He pushed two fingers deep inside of her, met hot, slippery friction, and almost lost it.

Not yet.

He focused on her, not the intense almost painful pressure in his groin. He used his tongue, his lips and fingers to pleasure her. Faster. Harder. Deeper.

"Now," she cried out. "I need you inside of me. Right. Now."

At her command he moved into position, poised at the entrance to paradise, close to detonating.

"I'm ready. So ready." She crossed her legs over his butt and urged him in.

Ian let loose the most powerful thrust of his life, buried himself to the hilt and stopped. His breath came like he'd just done a five mile run in full gear. His body tensed. One more like that and it'd be over.

"What are you waiting for?" Jaci asked.

Restraint. The ability to make the divine sensation of being embedded in the clasp of her sex last for all eternity.

But Jaci being Jaci she angled her hips, rocked beneath him and took what she needed.

Ian maintained a tenuous hold on his self-control by a single strand of a spider web as she rode his length. Until he had to give in to his release or implode. Decision made, Ian indulged his greatest desire and drove into her, repeatedly, barely holding out for her scream of completion, before he let go in the longest, most satisfying orgasm ever.

A tingly, joy-tinged, numbness seeped out from the depths of his core to his periphery, making him limp with rapture. Ian melted over top of Jaci.

Gratified and satisfied.

At peace.

Finally.

Jaci didn't mind the weight of a sated Ian making deep inhalation virtually impossible. Breathing was overrated, especially when even the slightest movement might interfere with her ability to savor precious moments of undisturbed bliss.

"I'll move in a minute. Promise," Ian mumbled into her shoulder.

"No rush." She glanced at his alarm clock. They had fourteen more minutes before dinner would be delivered. Who knew if she'd ever share this closeness with him again?

"I'm crushing you."

"In the best possible way." Still intimately connected, their bodies slick with the sweat of passion, and warmed in the aftermath of stellar sex. "Welcome home," she whispered.

"Welcome home sex was even better than I'd imagined." He rolled to his side, bringing Jaci with him.

"Makes me kind of disappointed I won't be heading back overseas."

"What?" He'd once told her serving in the military was all he'd ever wanted to do.

"Honorable discharge. I'm done."

"Because of your leg?" She slid her foot up his left calf, intending to wrap her thigh over her hip, and came in contact with irregular patches of bulging, puckered, indented skin.

Ian went rigid, didn't move or even breathe.

"I'm sorry." Jaci started to pull away. Ian let her. On top of his pain and disability, not being able to perform the work he loved had to be devastating. "You're a highly trained, decorated soldier with ten years of experience. Surely there has to be work available training new recruits or in administration."

He let a tense silence drag on between them, their closeness of a few minutes ago over.

"If I can't do the job I was originally hired for," he said the words quietly and succinctly, "I have no desire to remain on active duty."

"Do you have any idea what you'll do next?"

Ian didn't respond.

A sudden chill made her shiver. Jaci pulled the sheet up to her chin. This Ian was so different. Although she'd seen flashes of the warm, jocular man he'd been; when they were alone, his overall disposition vacillated between lustful desperation and brooding irritability. That combined with the nightmares she'd witnessed were a pretty good indication he suffered from some degree of P.T.S.D. Was he under a psychologist's care? Taking medication as prescribed? Now didn't feel like a good time to broach the topic.

Lying on her back, in the dark, staring up at the

ceiling, a foot of distance that may as well have been a
thousand miles separated them.

Jaci used the imposed isolation to think, to figure a
way to help him. His decreased body image—as evi-
denced by his unwillingness to remove his pants with
the light on and his reaction when she'd touched his bare
leg—could be worked on over time. What worried her
most was him being idle, sitting holed up in the condo,
day after day, night after night alone with his thoughts
and, what she anticipated were, horrible memories. Old
Ian was always in motion—except when they'd cuddled
on her couch. She missed that.

Focus. Ian needed to be kept busy, to have a reason
to get up and out every morning, to be a productive
member of society. He needed a job that could accommodate his physical limitations. Hey wait a minute.
Brilliant! "You know," Jaci said. "If you've got nothing
else lined up, maybe you'd want to work at the crisis
center. We're looking for a head of security and facility maintenance." A perfect solution for both of them.

"Ah, yes." Ian turned onto his back and folded his
hands behind his head. "Just what I've always aspired
to be, a glorified security guard slash janitor. Will I get
a badge and some official looking uniform? Maybe my
very own plunger?"

Jaci could do without his sarcasm.

"Thanks," he went on, sounding anything but thankful. "I guess someone like you probably sees that as a
great opportunity for someone like me."

Someone like him? What the heck was that supposed to mean?

"But I don't need your charity. I can find my own
job, a good job, something respectable that pays an en-

viable wage. I have skills, you know. I can do more than shoot people and fix things."

"Whoa." Jaci sat up. "Where'd that come from? Who said anything about you shooting anyone? And I wasn't offering you charity because I don't think you're capable of getting your own job. I offered a man with the exact skillset we're looking for, a job protecting our current sixty-seven residents who have been victimized and degraded, while they work to rebuild their lives. I was inviting you to be the first and only male member of our staff, the only man besides Justin who I'd trust to walk among our vulnerable clients, unsupervised."

Anger forced her out of bed. "As far as the job not being good enough or respectable enough or paying enough to suit you…" She flicked on the light, found her panties and slacks on the floor and jammed her feet into them. "A simple, 'not interested' would have sufficed. But let me tell you, I can't think of any job more respectable and rewarding than protecting women and children, than providing them with a safe environment in which they feel comfortable enough to let down their guard so they can learn and grow and regain their confidence. So they can go on to live happier more fulfilling lives." Ian was as much of a snob as Jerry the jerk. "And FYI, the job market in this area is saturated. I have fifty applicants begging to work for us. So before you make a snap decision that a job is unworthy of you, maybe you should check out the job description and wage scale."

He slid to the edge of the bed, looked like he wanted to get out, but stopped. Good. Because Jaci was so out of there.

"I didn't mean—"

Yes, he did. "In the end, life has to be about more than the titles and status you've achieved and the money you've amassed in your investment portfolio." She found her tank and sweater and put them on, to hell with the bra. "And if those are the things that matter most to you, you are obviously not the man I thought you were." She turned to leave.

"Jaci. Wait."

"Good luck, Ian," she said over her shoulder. "I hope you find what you're looking for." On her way through the living room Justin said, "Take it easy on him. He's having a tough time."

She knew that. Any fool could see it. Jaci picked up her nursing bag. But that didn't give him the right to insult someone who was trying to help him. She opened the door, fortuitous timing as it turned out, because Zach the delivery boy headed toward her.

"Two bags, just like you ordered, Miss J." He held them up. "And thanks for the mongo tip. You rock."

She smiled despite her lousy mood. "I'll take this one." She took the bag in his right hand. "Give me a minute to get to the elevator and you can deliver the other one to the condo I just came out of."

"Will do."

Her emotions churning, Jaci held it together through the elevator ride and the walk down the hall to find her home blessedly quiet. Jena sat on the couch in the darkened living room, her bare feet up on the coffee table a glass of white wine in hand. "I started without you."

After the day and evening she'd had, "I'll be caught up in two seconds." Jaci set the bag of food on the kitchen table, took the wine from the refrigerator and filled the glass Jena had left on the counter to the rim. Uh, oh. She bent to take a few sips before lifting it to avoid spillage.

Jena joined her in the kitchen. "You okay?"

No. She wasn't. Jaci burst into tears. "I'm sorry." She reached for a napkin. Jena had her own problems to deal with. She didn't need to be saddled with Jaci's.

"Don't be." Jena set her wineglass on the table. "Come here." She opened her arms and enveloped Jaci in a tight hug, which made her cry even harder.

"I'm so h-happy you're home," Jaci sobbed. "I m-missed you so m-much." Had been so sad and lonely after both Jena and Ian had deserted her without a word, within months of each other.

"Come sit on the couch." With her arm around Jaci's shoulder, Jena guided her in that direction.

"Wait," Jaci said. "Our wine."

"Heaven forbid we should forget the wine," Jena teased as she retrieved the glasses then met Jaci in the living room and sat beside her on the couch. "Spill."

Jaci glanced at her glass to see if she'd inadvertently tipped it.

"Not the wine, you boob. What has you so upset?"

Where to start? "Ian's back."

"Ian. The guy who kept you so busy you barely had time for your sister? The one we had the ménage with?"

Jaci glared at Jena. "That is not funny." She couldn't believe her sister's flippant response. "You left town. That rumor—and all the ones that'd followed—made my life hell for weeks." Especially because of Jerry's repeated demands that she accompany him to social events to do damage control. Like exaggerated, erroneous accounts of her sex life could possibly have a financial impact on a multi-billion-dollar corporation.

She'd expected it was all a ploy to dangle her in front of his eligible, well-connected business associates and refused to respond, which only served to anger him more.

"I'm sorry, hon," Jena said. "I was trying to lighten the mood and cheer you up like you've done for me every single time I've called you over the past months. Guess I'm not as good at it as you are. One more thing to add to the list."

Jaci responded like she always did when Jena put herself down. "Stop it. You're perfect." Because she was. She followed the words with a few hearty swigs of wine, welcoming the subsequent spread of warmth in her belly.

"Ian being back is good isn't it? You were crazy about him. At least until the—"

Jaci jerked up her hand. "Don't say it."

"Never again." Jena pretended to lock her lips with a key. As if.

"He said it was all a big misunderstanding," Jaci explained. "A bunch of guys acting like idiots, combined with the picture of us at the Fourth of July barbecue two years ago, and the twin fantasy run amok."

"Ew." Jena scrunched her face in revulsion. "Men are pigs."

Jaci took a more ladylike sip of wine, smiled, and relaxed into the back of the sofa. "That's what he said."

"When was the last time you ate?" Jena asked.

"Lunch. And some stale crackers at Ian's." Which she'd surely worked off in bed.

"We'd better get some food in you before you pass out," Jena said, taking Jaci's glass—which was almost empty. Okay, maybe the last sip hadn't been as ladylike as she'd thought.

Over dinner they talked about Ian, Jaci's work and the crisis center. Every time Jaci tried to steer the conversation in Jena's direction—to find out where she'd been, how long she planned to stick around, and the twenty-five-million-dollar questions, who was her babies' daddy and had she come home to tell him, she found her wine topped off and the conversation veering back in her direction.

She yawned. "I have a long day tomorrow and I'm scheduled to be at the crisis center from four to nine." After visiting a packed schedule of patients.

"I know why you're working so hard."

"Because I have two jobs that I love and can't decide between them so I do both?" Although the fact she was paid to be a community health nurse made that one slightly more appealing at the moment since most of her available cash went to purchase things for the residents at the crisis center.

"No," Jena said.

"So I can have the weekend and afternoons off next week to spend with you. I have us booked for manis, and pedis Saturday morning. Celia is coming to do our hair and makeup—" identically, which was imperative "—at four. The car is coming at six. We'll be at the benefit ready to meet and greet by six-thirty. Sunday brunch at the Inn at Elmsford then we'll relax and play with the girls. Monday shopping. Tuesday into the city for dinner and a show."

"And you're going to try to fill up every moment we have together so we don't talk about it."

"I'm not the only one avoiding certain discussions," Jaci shot back. "I know. You want to talk? Let's start with where you've been? Why you left? Who's the—?"

"I'm the guest. So I decide what we talk about." Jena adjusted her napkin in her lap primly and spoke like her words were written in an etiquette guide somewhere. "And I want to talk about you and who you're going to marry."

Yeah, well Jaci would rather solve quadratic equations. And she hated math. She pushed her plate away, too full, or, more likely, too unsettled to eat another bite. "I refuse to be forced into marriage." She gave her standard answer.

"What about Ian? You sure seemed to like him enough at one point."

True. But she'd only seen the fun, let's-hang-out-and-do-enjoyable-things-to-each-other's-bodies side of him. "He's changed." And while the physical parts of him still very much appealed to her, his transformation into an overbearing, lecturing, worrywart who no longer worked with the army and would be home, nosing into her business, all the time, did not. "I'm torn between advertising for a husband on a couple of billboards around town, just to see Jerry's reaction, and telling him to shove the damn money, I don't want it." But while she made a decent living and had invested enough of the inheritance she'd received from her mother to live comfortably for the rest of her life, a large infusion of cash would eliminate the need for her to continually contribute her personal money to keep the crisis center going.

With her portion of the fifty million dollar trust due to be distributed when she and Jena turned twenty-five, if they were happily married at the time, Jaci could open more centers in other areas of the county, provide more services to help more women.

Jaci cleared her dishes and placed them in the sink so she could have her back to Jena when she shared her present plan. "There's a guy up on the tenth floor. We speak in passing. He's not bad to look at. Investment banker. Dresses nice. Brandon says he's a generous tipper and he couldn't recall seeing him with the same woman more than once. I'm considering offering him a deal. Marriage for money. A straight business transaction." Payment for husbandly services rendered to include acting adoringly at public functions, letting Jaci come and go as she pleased without question, and relieving any physical urges somewhere else—discreetly—so neither of them got too content with their living arrangement. Because five years to the day from when she put her signature on a marriage certificate she'd put it on a divorce petition. Her penance served, she would return to her life of independence.

Jena's fork clanged on her plate. "No, Jaci. You can't marry a complete stranger. There's someone out there for you, we just need to find him."

Sweet, naïve Jena still held out hope for true love. A myth. And even if she did manage to get all starry-eyed over some guy, how long until things changed? Until love turned to tolerance turned to dissatisfaction and abuse? "I haven't found a suitable man in twenty-four years—" although old Ian had come close "—and I'm somehow supposed to fall in love in ninety days." Impossible. Although, "If me marrying someone I don't know is the problem, I guess I could always ask Justin," she said, thinking out loud.

Jena choked on a sip of wine.

Very interesting. "I forgot. You used to have a crush on him." Is that why she'd come back, to make a play for Justin? They were, after all, both in the same race against the calendar.

"Well I certainly don't anymore." Jena added her dishes to the sink. "You can have him." Her words lacked conviction. "He doesn't want me anyway."

"I'm ashamed of us," Jaci said. "Talking like any man would do." They both knew firsthand the importance of vetting out a kind, easily managed, even-tempered partner.

"Jerald seems to think so. As long as it's someone he chooses for us."

And he'd become even more aggressive in that regard of late. "As far as I'm concerned, being a friend or business associate of Jerry's warrants instant disqualification from the potential-marriageable-male-pool. But," Jaci said, wrapping her arm around Jena's shoulders. "Let's keep that between you and me until after we take their generous contributions for the Women's Crisis Center Saturday night."

"Deal," Jena said on a nod with a conspiratory smile.

"You are a major-league jerk," Justin said, barging into Ian's room without knocking.

"Five years as my friend and you're just figuring that out?" Ian had forgotten all he had on was a pair of briefs until he turned to see Justin staring at his leg.

"Looks like it got stuck in a wood chipper and some mad scientist stitched you up."

Because he'd lost tissue and muscle in the explosion. Burns. Skin grafts. Multiple debridements. And the surgeries to repair his shattered bones. "I'm guessing all the surgeons who pieced me back together would wave their fancy degrees in outrage over that statement." Ian reached for a pair of sweatpants.

"It's better than if you didn't have it at all."

Ian wasn't so sure. Maybe he should have let them hack it off. Maybe adjusting to a prosthetic would have been easier than putting up with the constant pain and stiffness and damn unpredictability of what remained of his leg.

"Stop," Justin said. "I've had enough of you feeling

sorry for yourself. You're alive, Ian. Thousands of soldiers never made it home and you did."

That was the problem. "Why? Why me? My men had wives and kids. Families and friends who loved them." Why was Ian chosen to live over them? His brothers. His family for the past ten years. He didn't deserve the honor, didn't want it, and given the opportunity he'd have traded places with any one of his dead buddies in an instant, with all of them.

"You have family and friends who love you, too, you idiot."

"Why, Justin," he teased. "I'm touched."

"Joke around all you want." He picked up a framed family photo taken about a dozen years ago from Ian's dresser. "Your mother and your sisters were wrong to turn their backs on you when you enlisted in the army."

"If you follow in your father's footsteps you will wind up dead on foreign soil just like he did. I refuse to live in a constant state of anxiety. Worrying. Obsessing over news reports of what's happening with the war. Stressing when I don't hear from you. Dreading the sight of a pair of officers in their dress uniforms showing up on my doorstep. I can't go through that again, Ian. And neither can your sisters."

"But that doesn't mean they don't love you, that they wouldn't have gone to the hospital if you'd called them."

"A nurse contacted my mother when I arrived at the army regional medical center in Germany." As next of kin since, his prognosis grave, there'd been concern he wouldn't make it through the night. He hesitated, the next part difficult to admit. But this was Justin. "She requested to have her name and phone number removed from my file."

Unconditional love was a thing of fairytales.

"When I arrived back in the U.S.," Ian continued, "a social worker convinced me to call her so she wouldn't worry. Mom told me I'd made the decision to join the army on my own, and I could suffer the consequences of that decision on my own. As far as she's concerned, her only son died on his eighteenth birthday." The day he'd enlisted.

"Well that deserves a one-way ticket into the depths of hell." Justin slammed the picture frame, face down, on the dresser. "But don't take your anger out on Jaci. I've never seen her as upset as she was in the weeks after you left, even after your disappearing act, you coward. And yet she's still talking to you and obviously still cares for you. You should be on your knees thanking God you have another chance with a woman like her. Instead you insult her and piss on one of the things that mean the most to her."

Did she still care for him? After everything he'd done to push her away? And why did Justin have to go ahead and put the idea of a second chance into his head? "I did not—"

"You damn well did, too," Justin yelled. "I can find my own job, a good job, a respectable job," he mimicked Ian.

"Got nothing better to do with your time than listen in on my *private* conversations?"

Justin didn't acknowledge that Ian had even spoken. "You basically screamed out that the center she'd donated huge sums of her own money to create, a tribute to her mother meant to benefit the cause dearest to her heart, one she works tirelessly to run and promote, isn't respectable."

That wasn't it at all. Ian had reacted—poorly as it turned out—to the idea of working for her and getting paid by her, because how could a woman as smart, successful, and wealthy as Jaci respect a man who was totally dependent on her emotionally, physically, and financially?

"Have you ever been there?" Justin asked.

Ian felt on par with the sludge in a latrine after chili night. "No."

"I'm happy to have you home, man. And I'm willing to give you time to get your happy-go-lucky back on. But I will not stand by and watch you hurt my best female friend, again."

Ian feared his happy-go-lucky was gone for good. "Exactly what do you plan to do about it?" He clenched his fists, needed a good fight. He and Justin were evenly matched. Bring it on.

"I'll shoot you in the head and claim it was a mercy killing."

Ian deflated. "Yeah. You do that." A month or two ago he would have welcomed a bullet to the head.

"For the record, Jaci offered me the job last month after some jackoff got drunk and shattered the window in the reception area with a chair, trying to get to his ex."

A protective instinct flared inside of him. "They didn't have security glass?"

"It was supposed to be. Jaci didn't know what to look for. Turns out the contractor had ripped her off. The plumbers and electricians overcharge. As much as she hated to admit it, the crisis center needs a more regular male presence than me showing up two evenings a week when men are let in for couples counseling. We interviewed a guy last week that was the best so far. I'm going to suggest she hire him."

"Don't."

"Why?" Justin laughed. "You think you have a chance at that job, now? You'd have better luck applying at the lingerie shop down at the mall."

Maybe. But he didn't like the idea of some slacker providing half-assed protection at Jaci's crisis center. The thought of Merlene's boyfriend showing up, gunning for Jaci, heated the blood coursing through his veins. He owed her. For her letter. For still caring about him. For bringing him back to life. He could help out, at least temporarily, until he finished with physical therapy and was ready to move on.

CHAPTER SIX

IAN spent the next day more on edge than usual, pacing, fidgeting, unable to find a comfortable position. Justin had convinced him to give Jaci the night to cool down. In the light of a new day, Ian wasn't convinced that had been the best course of action. She was gone by the time he'd gone down to her condo that morning. And her sister's voice through the closed door sounded so much like her it was as if Jaci herself had told him she'd already left for work. In what, he'd wondered, since the car she'd been using was still wedged under a tree in the condo parking lot. Jena didn't know. And Jaci hadn't answered one of his calls.

Granted she was at work, but not even a quick, "I'm busy"? Things were not looking good.

After his third time calling Jaci's condo, Jena took pity on him and divulged where Jaci would be at four o'clock, which was why Ian stood on the sidewalk in front of the Women's Crisis Center, freshly shaved and showered, in dress pants that were at least a size too big—he knew he'd lost some weight since his injury, but until today hadn't realized how much—and his only designer white button-down dress shirt.

On the border of a gentrification-in-progress neighborhood, to the far right stood luxury, soon-to-be waterfront condos, while to the immediate left were rundown, mostly abandoned storefronts. It looked like the nondescript building the center had taken over had once been a massive corner bank.

Through a large plate glass window framed by an artsy interpretation of colorful flowers and meandering vines, Ian saw a young, meek-looking woman sitting all alone behind a reception counter with sliding panes of glass at her chest level. Ian tried the heavy glass door. Locked. Good. Then a buzzer sounded, followed by a click, and Ian could open the door without one question asked or answered through the dented, partially dislodged intercom speaker to his left.

That would have to be fixed. He started a mental list. The lobby was small, with six matching chairs—not old, not new—a small table with well-read magazines neatly fanned on top, and a plastic storage container filled to overflowing with children's toys. It kind of looked like a doctor's office waiting room, only the pale yellow walls, colorful artwork, and the table with fresh coffee and pre-wrapped, single-serving food items/snacks made it feel more welcoming.

"May I help you?" the woman asked with a smile.

"Is Jaci in?"

"Who may I say is asking?"

"Ian Eddelton."

The receptionist spoke quietly into the phone. Nodded. Then looked up at Ian. "She said to go away, Mr. Eddelton."

Did he honestly expect she'd welcome him with open arms? "Please tell her I'm here to apply for the head of security and facility maintenance position."

She relayed the message.

"Miss Piermont said to tell you the position has been filled."

His insides felt suddenly hollow when the hope and anticipation that'd built up all afternoon, evacuated the premises. Because the more he'd thought about it, while awake most of the night and alone most of the day, the more he'd realized he wanted the job and the opportunity to get out of the condo to do something meaningful with his days, to earn a regular paycheck, and, to be honest, to see Jaci every day.

At least until he moved on.

But he'd blown it.

Ian stood there, contemplating his next move.

Threaten to break down the flimsy wooden door and search until he found Jaci. Because job or no job, he needed to apologize for last night's misunderstanding.

Take a self-guided tour around the outside of the building to search out another way to access the interior.

Plead his case to the hopefully easily persuadable young woman looking up at him questioningly and convince her to let him in without violence.

Deciding option three was the way to go, Ian planned out his appeal. But before he had the chance to put any of his eloquent, carefully chosen words to use, the flimsy wooden door opened to reveal Jaci. She wore royal blue scrub pants with matching rubber clogs, and a pink scrub top with cartoon characters on it.

She looked tired and inconvenienced.

Not a good combination.

But when the outside door to the lobby opened and a small woman dressed in baggy, worn clothes, who couldn't be more than sixteen, walked in carrying a small baby, Jaci managed a warm, welcoming smile.

"Come in. I expect the doctor any minute. Have you been here before?"

The woman didn't look up from the floor.

"You're safe here," Jaci said, approaching the woman cautiously, compassionately. "Can I help you with your bag?"

Ian stepped out of the way. At his movement, the woman flinched and shifted her body to cover and protect her baby.

"It's okay." Jaci tried to calm her. "That's my friend, Ian. If he makes you uncomfortable, I'll ask him to leave."

In that moment, Ian realized just how big a compliment she'd paid him by trusting him to walk amongst the center's vulnerable clients unsupervised. He'd had no idea of the magnitude of that responsibility until he'd experienced that young woman's fear of a man she didn't even know.

A beat up black and rust-covered Honda skidded to a stop half onto the curb.

The woman gasped. "Please. He will be so angry. I seek refuge," she said in heavily accented English. That's when Ian caught a glimpse of her swollen eye, split lip and bruised cheek.

A dark-haired man, possibly of Mexican descent, jumped out of the car and stormed toward the front door. Jaci wrapped her arm around the woman and guided her into the center. "Andrea, call the police. Carla, I need your help," she called out.

The baby in the woman's arms cried out.

"Loosen your hold," Jaci encouraged, her voice calm. "No one is going to harm you or your baby."

Damn straight. Not as long as Ian was around. He hurried outside eager to meet the low-life, abuser, who was in for a little abuse himself if he didn't back the hell off. "Stop right there," Ian commanded.

The man halted about five feet from Ian like he'd collided with an invisible wall. So there were some functioning brain cells in his head after all.

"That woman," the man said, his English only marginally better than the woman's. "I saw her in the window. I am here to take her home."

Not a chance. "She's requested to stay for a while."

"She is my Maria, my girlfriend." He stepped forward. "The baby is mine. I take care of them."

"Back off." Ian stood tall and crossed his arms over his chest no-way-you're-getting-past-me style. "One look at your girlfriend's face and I can see how well you take care of her."

The man exploded in rapid fire Spanish.

"*No hablo español*, buddy. English."

"What happened to her face?" the man screamed. No way could he have faked the anguish in his voice or the complete and utter devastation on his face. More Spanish. "Did she go to her brother for money?" Spanish. "I told her not to go."

Whoa. Pay attention, Ice. Assess. Evaluate. Things were often not as they appeared to be.

"I need to see her." The distraught man, probable teenager, who stood a good foot and a half shorter than Ian and looked to weigh no more than Jaci, tried to push past him. A sure sign he'd moved past thinking clearly. "I need to see she is okay."

"Hold on." Ian stopped him.

"I'm going to kill her brother," the man yelled, twisting away, pacing back and forth.

Ian looked around. "You probably don't want to be

saying that out loud in front of witnesses. And what good will you do your girl and your kid in jail?"

"No more than I'm doing now." He jammed his fists into the pockets of his loose-fitting jeans so hard Ian half expected them to slide down to his knees. "There is no work for me. Our rent is late. Soon we will have no place to live."

Poor kid. "You sure you didn't touch her?" Ian asked.

"Last night we had a fight. I yelled. I said things I should not have."

Ian could relate.

"But I would never hit her." His eyes filled with tears. He wiped them away. Embarrassed. "I love her."

Ian felt sorry for the guy, down on his luck, with a wife and kid to support. It hit home a truth: No matter how bad you think you have it, there's always someone worse off than you are. "Look. Get out of here. The police are on their way. I'll talk to them." Ian didn't know if the man was in the U.S. legally or illegally. A run in with the law could make things even worse for him. But…Ian stared into the man's eyes, "If I find out you lied to me, and you are in fact the one responsible for hurting Maria, I will hunt you down and you will wish you'd stuck around to deal with the police."

"What will happen to Maria?" he asked, panicked, glancing frantically up and down the street.

"We'll take care of her and the baby," Jaci said from the doorway.

Shoot, exactly how long had she been standing there?

"They are both in with our doctor now," Jaci went on.

The man's eyes went wide. "The baby. She was hurt, too?" He wobbled. Ian reached out to steady him.

"Maria is scared and she's not talking. But the baby's cry is strong, which is good, and she's moving her arms and legs. As soon as Maria lets us examine her and the baby, we'll know more. If the doctor thinks either one needs to be evaluated in the Emergency Room, we'll transport them."

The man groaned and dropped his face into his hands. "I can't leave them. I don't want to live my life without them."

Ian glanced at Jaci and understood exactly how the guy felt. Lord help him.

"She's upset." Jaci walked onto the sidewalk. "I give you my word I will not leave here tonight until she and the baby are settled."

Of course she wouldn't. As tired as she looked, Jaci put everyone else's needs ahead of her own.

"Will you ask her to call me?"

Jaci smiled. "Yes."

"I will come for her tomorrow morning. When do you open?" he asked.

"You are welcome to come by any time tomorrow, but I can't guarantee she'll be ready to talk to you."

"Then I will wait all day if I have to."

Not alone he wouldn't. "You promise to stay away from Maria's brother tonight, and I'll meet you here at nine o'clock tomorrow morning," Ian said. "We can look into finding you a job while you wait."

"*Gracias*," he said to Ian. "Thank you." He turned to leave then stopped. "You will tell Maria I love her," he said to Jaci. "And ask her to kiss our little angel for me."

Jaci set her hand on the man's shoulder. "I will."

Ian hung around to talk to the police who arrived with the smell of Maria's boyfriend's exhaust still in the air. Ian explained what'd happened. Jaci came out to share that Maria had gone hysterical when she was told the police wanted to speak with her. Thankfully they didn't push the issue.

After the policemen drove off and Jaci returned to work, Ian stood on the curb, looking toward the horizon, no reason to go inside, not ready to head home.

"You handled that situation exactly the way I'd want my head of security to handle it," Jaci called out from behind him. "The job's yours if you still want it."

Ian's spirits lifted instantly. He turned to her. "I thought you said the position was filled."

"I lied. But I can't in good conscience let you walk away when you are what the crisis center needs." She held out some papers. "Here's the job description, salary and benefits. Look them over and let me know—"

He decided not to tell her it'd only be temporary lest she rescind the offer. "I'll take it." To bring the building up to spec and work up security protocols. Then he'd search out his replacement and would not leave until the new guy was trained and performing to Ian's high standards.

Jaci didn't look happy or relieved. In fact she showed no emotion at all. "Fine. Please put finding someone to drain and clean up our parking lot and deal with the flooded vehicles at the top of your list."

"Roger that."

She turned to walk back into the building. "I have to get to work."

"I'm sorry about last night," he called after her. Not the sex part, but the misunderstanding afterwards.

"You should be."

He jogged to the door and opened it for her. "How are you getting around?" She'd been with him until almost eight last evening, and she'd left for work before seven that morning. Did car rental places open before seven in the morning?

"The home care agency I work for provides visit cars for the nurses. I took a taxi to work and a taxi here."

"How will you get home?"

"If I'm done by the time Carla has to leave she'll drop me off. Or I'll call a cab."

He hated the idea of her being driven around by strangers. "I'll hang around and give you a ride."

"Thank you. But it's not necessary. I won't be done before nine and depending on what happens with our newest arrival, I may not be able to leave until well after that."

"I've got nothing better to do." He walked into the building it was now his responsibility to maintain and secure, feeling an unexpected sense of pride. "It'll give me a chance to fill out this paperwork and look around."

"C'mon, then. I'll introduce you."

Finally. An invite into the inner sanctum.

"Then Carla can give you a tour."

On Saturday night, ten minutes after they were supposed to have left for the yacht club, Jena rushed into the living room. "I'm sorry." She fumbled with an earring. "I thought I heard Annie stirring. Have you seen my shoes?"

Jaci held up a second pair of the exquisite pumps that graced her own feet. "You look beautiful."

Splurging on matching style designer liquid shine sequined, one-shoulder, fishtail gowns turned out to be worth every one of the many dollars spent. The blue of Jena's dress played up her slightly paler complexion and eyes. And Jaci loved the way the champagne color of her own dress shimmered against her skin tone. The ruched waist accented their slim figures, before flowing down to pool on the floor at their feet.

"Absolute perfection," Mrs. Calvin said with a clap of her hands. "Don't you worry about the twins. You go out and have a wonderful evening. They are in good hands."

Three pairs of hands as Mrs. Calvin had brought two of her pre-teen granddaughters to assist her. Not that she needed the help. According to Jena, she'd raised five children with a husband who was away on business for weeks at a time. Yikes.

"I have complete confidence," Jena said. But she rattled off several reminders including when the twins would likely be waking up, to make sure to keep them each in the same colored outfits as they have on, and to check the temperature of the formula before giving the girls their bottles, anyway. Standing in the doorway she said, "I'll have my phone with me every minute. If you have any questions or anything seems hinky, call me right away."

"We'll be fine, dear." Mrs. Calvin tried to reassure Jena. "But I'll be sure to call if I need you."

"Thank you," Jena said. Still not leaving.

Jaci wanted to tell her it was okay if she didn't want to go. Regardless of how much she needed Jena there. She could work something else out. Would have to. She let out a breath. Jena had to come first. "You don't have to come," Jaci said. "I've attended fundraisers without you before." None as important as this one.

"I want a night out. I *need* a night out," Jena insisted. "I have spent the day psyching myself up for the confrontation with Jerald. If I wimp out all my practiced comebacks and your wonderful pep talks will have been wasted. I think if you pry my hand off the frame of the door I'll be good to go."

Jaci looked down to see Jena did in fact have a white-knuckled grip on the doorframe. She covered Jena's cold hand with her own. "Are you sure?"

Jena nodded.

So she inserted two fingers between Jena's palm and the door, broke the hold, and they were off. "Hinky? Did I honestly just hear you use the word hinky?"

They laughed.

"I forgot how nice it feels to get all glammed up in expensive clothes," Jena said in the elevator, pinching the diamond studded J necklace their mother had given each of them on their tenth birthday.

"Jerry always said, 'You have to spend money to make money.' In this case, a few thousand dollars on clothing, accessories and appearances will hopefully net the crisis center a few hundred thousand dollars in donations."

"I promise to dance whenever I am asked, to engage in tantalizing conversation, and be my most enchanting self to benefit your cause."

"You're the best," Jaci said. And she meant it.

The limo awaited them right outside the front door. On the way to the yacht club, Jena indulged in a glass of champagne, to calm her nerves. Jaci declined needing to stay alert.

"I asked Jerry to show up half an hour early so we can corner him before our guests start arriving," Jaci said.

"How'd you get him to agree to that?"

"I told him there was someone special I wanted him to meet. Now pay attention." She reviewed their schedules for the evening. "At exactly twenty minutes before ten—"

"I take the rear stairs by the kitchen and meet you in

the upstairs bathroom outside ballroom C," Jena said. "Where we'll exchange dresses and lives and you'll go off on yet another secret caper while I stay behind and pretend to be you. I close down the event, I take the limo home, and we meet up in the kitchen for a celebratory job-well-done toast at midnight."

God willing things would go that smoothly.

"I love the quiet, elegant beauty of a fully decorated ballroom before the ambiance is defiled by a swarm of people looking for their seats and disturbing their place settings," Jena said.

"The centerpieces look even nicer than I'd imagined." An abundance of white dendrobium orchids atop clear glass pedestals so guests could converse across the table without obstruction.

"They're magnificent, and so are you," Jena said, pulling Jaci into a hug. "I'm so proud of you and all you've accomplished in three short years."

"Jena?" Jerry's voice killed their touching moment. Jaci glanced at the Movado bangle watch she'd retrieved from her safety deposit box for the occasion. Right on time as always.

"Jena, honey, is it really you?"

"No Jerry, she's a living, breathing figment of your over-active imagination," Jaci deadpanned.

As usual he ignored her and pulled Jena out of her arms and into his. "I was hoping you'd show up tonight. Preston will be so pleased." Right onto the business of marrying them off, he stepped back, took out his phone and started to text.

Jena grabbed the phone from his hand. "Stop."

Had she had a mirror handy, Jaci was certain the look of shock on Jerry's face would have been replicated on hers, albeit a prettier version. Torn between asking,

"Who are you and what have you done with Jena?" and yelling, "Go, Jen!" she opted for quiet admiration instead. Apparently the changing her baby sister had done while away was not limited to diapers.

"Don't text Preston, or William, or Jonathan Michael Randolph the fourth," Jena said. "I am not nor will I ever be interested in any one of them."

"They're good men, Jena. I'd like for at least one of my sisters to make a decent match." He took that moment to finally acknowledge Jaci's presence with a glare.

"Why don't you define decent match, Jerry?" Jaci asked, taunting him by using the nickname he despised. "Is it someone who will love us and be faithful to us and never lift a hand to us like we deserve? Or is it an acquaintance of yours who made a deal with the devil for full access to our trust funds?"

"Maybe you'd better take this little family reunion to a more private location." Ian joined their group. In a tuxedo. Va-va-voom… Words escaped her. Well, not all words. Hot, sexy, handsome, powerful, kissable, huggable and the like all stuck around, leaving her the vocabulary of a phone sex operator.

Jena took one look at her and then Ian and stuck out her hand. "You must be Ian. It's a pleasure to finally meet you face to face."

Ian shook her hand.

That gave Jaci the chance she needed to regroup. "What are you doing here?" she asked Ian. And why did his unexpected appearance fill her with so many conflicting emotions? Happiness. Guilt. Relief. Dread.

"I'm working security with Justin."

Jena's hand went to her throat. "Justin's here?"

"You put that troublemaker on the event payroll?" Jerry asked.

"He is not a troublemaker," Jena and Jaci said in unison, like they had so many times growing up, then pointed at each other and raced to add, "Pinch poke you owe me a Coke. Stand and holler you owe me a dollar."

While they laughed like goofball school girls, Jerry asked Ian, "Who the hell are you?"

"Ian Eddelton." Ian held out his hand. "Veteran U.S. Army recently returned from Iraq."

Jerry's eyes narrowed. "You." Recognition dawned. "Your lies have made it significantly more difficult for me to find suitable men to marry my sisters."

"Actually they've made me quite popular," Jaci quipped.

Ian joined Jerry in a double glare.

Jaci held up both hands in surrender. "I'm just telling it like it is. Heading into the weekend my voicemail fills up." Because she usually took weekend call to earn extra money and her co-workers called in report for any anticipated problems and any patients requiring visits.

"I said *suitable* men," Jerry snapped.

"The rumors that made their way back to the states were all a big misunderstanding," Ian explained. "I've never met Jena in person until tonight, but she was in the picture I had of Jaci. Men in a warzone tend to go a little crazy at the sight of a beautiful woman in a bikini. Make it two identical—"

"The twin fantasy," Jerry said with a nod.

"Honestly," Jena said in full dudgeon. "At times men are such vile creatures." She held out the picture of the twins. "This is what we're here to discuss so let's get to it."

Jaci leaned in, cupped her hand around Jena's ear

and whispered, "Whatever has gotten into you, I like it." Watching Jena stand up to Jerry for the first time ever was a sight to behold.

Jerry looked at it. Confused. "What are those?" he asked.

"Your nieces." Jena stood tall then looked at Jaci. "I'm a mother now. I am responsible for two little girls. If I can't stand up for myself, how am I going to stand up for them?"

"This is why you ran off? To get married?" Jerry asked. Incredulous.

"No," Jena snapped. "What does my giving birth to twins have to do with getting married?"

And Jerry went off…on Jaci. "This is all *your* fault," he yelled.

"This is between you and me, Jerald." Jena tried to redirect Jerry's anger. It never worked. So Jaci did what she always did. She came back fighting.

"You know, not everything is my fault and it's about time you stopped blaming me."

Ian put an arm around her shoulder. "I'll get her. You get him," he said to Jena, then forcibly guided her in the direction of the coatroom.

"Let me go."

"Not until you're in a spot where photographers can't snap your picture, and microphones and nosey ears can't hear you." They stopped back by the banquet manager's office. "Here." He released her. "Let him have it."

Jaci turned and did just that. "Trust me, Jerry. No one wishes mom and dad were here more than me. Because then I wouldn't have to deal with you."

"But they're not here, are they?" He flattened invisible wrinkles from an arm of his tux and adjusted a cufflink. "Why is that?"

"Their deaths were not my fault." It'd taken years of expensive therapy sessions before she could sound confident uttering those words, especially since she still didn't believe them. "I am sorry dad lost his temper with me and grabbed me so hard he dislocated my shoulder." Because she'd broken curfew yet again. It'd started out as their typical row until mom had shown up.

"I am sorry mom tried to intervene and he flung her to the side so hard she fell and hit her head on the marble fireplace and sustained a traumatic brain injury." Why hadn't she gone to bed at ten and stayed there? Like she always did.

"I am sorry that overwhelmed by pain and the sight of my mother lying motionless on the floor, with blood oozing from her head, the public image of the then head of Piermont Enterprises was not first and foremost in my mind when I told the police the truth about what happened, rather than lying to save face like you wanted me to. I'm sorry dad was brought in for questioning and suffered a massive, fatal heart attack while waiting for his attorney." Alone in a holding cell. On a dirty cement floor.

"You're not to blame," Jena said.

Jerry remained quiet.

"Jena and I were teenagers when things got really bad. You were twenty-three," Jaci yelled at Jerry. "A full-grown man. Everyone in that house knew what went on. Yet you did nothing to help my mother." Because he'd never thought her mom was good enough for their dad. Imagine, a Piermont marrying the bourgeois daughter of a plumber. Regardless of the fact she'd put herself through college and graduate school and had earned a sought after spot on the management team of dad's company.

Until she'd resigned to marry her prince charming and raise their little princesses.

"Maybe if you weren't such a pain in the ass," Jerry yelled back at Jaci, "Dad wouldn't have been so mad all the time and he wouldn't have taken his anger out on your mother."

A widespread misperception which she noticed Jena did not dispute. But in her own way, Jaci had actually been trying to protect her mother. By acting out and drawing daddy's ire. And it'd been working, too. Mom and dad had actually seemed happier for those last two years. Jaci's guess, dad rarely denied her approval to go out with friends or to a party, because he looked forward to her coming home after curfew, with alcohol on her breath, and a mouth full of sarcastic, disrespectful remarks.

She imagined him sitting in the leather chair behind his desk, smoking his imported cigar, watching the clock in eager anticipation, waiting for the front door to open.

And let there be no doubt, Jaci received the full force of his anger. Her mom may have given up the fight, but Jaci had been full of fire.

Oh the irony of mom suffering a life-altering blow to the head as a result of trying to protect Jaci who was indirectly trying to protect her, then lingering for years with significant cognitive deficits and physical impairments, requiring round the clock nursing care. A daily reminder of what had happened, of how, in the end, Jaci hadn't done enough.

Jena looked at her with sadness.

Jerry looked at her with disgust.

Ian looked at her with a mix of shock and pity that made her want to scream.

Jaci fought off tears. She wasn't that angry, misguided, rebellious teenager anymore. She was a philanthropist, as well known for her heritage as her work with the Women's Crisis Center she'd founded. "I paid two hundred and fifty dollars to have my makeup professionally done for tonight, and I'll be damned if I'm going to screw it up before my guests arrive."

"Why do you always look for someone to blame?" Jena asked Jerry.

He didn't have to look far because Jaci was always in his sights.

"If anyone is to blame for pushing me to lose myself in the arms of a man I cared about," Jena went on, "it's you," she pointed at Jerry's chest, "and your relentless attempts to foist your business associates on me, more concerned about who would most favorably impact your long term financial plan than what is in my best interest."

Jaci held in a cheer. Jena had practiced that line during their pedicures and had hoped for an opportunity to use it.

"Well you sure fixed me by going out and getting yourself pregnant," Jerry said in the sarcastic tone he usually reserved for Jaci. "But you'd be surprised what a man will put up with for twenty-five million dollars." He slid a look at Jaci as if to imply one might even take her on.

"Like that's my only allure," Jena said.

"It is now," Jerry answered. "Who do you think will want you with another man's pair of squalling brats? Do you even know who the father is? Or have you turned into your sister, running around town with a change of underwear and a toothbrush in your purse?"

Jena gasped.

Jaci had heard that insult before.

Ian grabbed Jerry by the bowtie and yanked him close enough to kiss. "You obviously know very little about Jaci you ill-mannered, disrespectful, lousy excuse for a brother."

"Stepbrother," Jerry choked out like there may have been a little airway compression going on.

Jaci found herself disconcertingly pleased by that.

"If Jena is anything like Jaci," Ian continued, "any man with half a working brain would be honored to marry her because she's sweet and caring, beautiful and smart, hard-working and dedicated."

Jaci's breath caught. Did he honestly believe that?

"Thank you," Jena said quietly, looking down at the floor.

Ian released Jerry who sucked in a deep breath. "I'm done with the both of you," he said. "When you don't meet the terms of your trust funds, I will happily write out checks to each and every one of the charities dad designated. I'm sure they'll be delighted."

"Well before you succumb to hand cramps from all that check writing," Jaci said. "I read in the newspaper Piermont Enterprises is committed to the future of the Women's Crisis Center and has pledged to match the total donations we receive tonight." She had a copy of the front page article stashed away as insurance. "You'd better get yourself ready to write a check with a lot of zeroes on it because Millicent Parks coordinated a silent auction for us this year that's estimated to bring in half a million dollars, the dear. She's donated several pieces of jewelry and artwork from her private collection." Unbeknownst to her husband, which was another reason Jaci had wanted Justin around. Although Mrs. Parks had provided Jaci with a notarized letter from

her attorney and documentation of her personal owner-
ship to make sure there would be no repercussions for
Jaci or the crisis center, Jaci was glad to have backup
on hand just in case.

Jerry walked away without a word.

"If you don't pay or your check doesn't clear," she
called after him, "I'll grant an interview request to one
of the many magazines, newspapers, and television talk
shows who continue to get in touch with me year after
year. Whichever one offers me the most money. And I'll
tell all." Since odds were around fifty-fifty she'd meet
the terms of her trust fund, and Mrs. Parks wouldn't
be around to assist on future events, Jaci needed every
penny she could get this year.

A slight hesitation in his step was the only indication he'd heard her.

CHAPTER SEVEN

Iᴀɴ spotted Jaci instantly, in a rare moment alone, standing by the corner of the dance floor, her shimmery champagne-colored gown an enticingly elegant wrapper covering her delectable treats. He'd had no idea how difficult tonight would be, standing on the sidelines, watching her laugh and flirt as dozens of men, old and young alike, touched her and danced with her, and held her much too close.

He absolutely hated seeing her with other men.

To take his mind off it, he'd actually scoped out a few locations from which he could easily pick them off one by one. If only he'd brought his silencer. If only this were a warzone and the men were targets of an op, and not the targets of Jaci's hobnobbing with high society's elite agenda, to raise money for her crisis center. "Hey, beautiful." He snuck up behind her. "I'm on break. You promised me a dance."

She stiffened, just a touch, but enough for him to notice, before turning to face him. Her eyes gave her away. Something was up.

"Certainly." She held out her hand formally and he led her to the dance floor.

"Are you enjoying yourself?" he asked to make conversation, watching her closely.

"Always," she responded without elaborating, her smile too bright. Forced.

He took her in his arms and swayed to the tunes coming from the ten piece orchestra. She wore Jaci's dress. Felt like Jaci, moved like Jaci, even smelled like Jaci.

But Ian's intuition rarely failed him. He leaned back to take a closer look at her. "Jena?" he asked.

She laughed—a little too loud. "After all the time we've spent together you can't tell me apart from my sister?"

So that's how she wanted to play it? Fine. He'd flush out the truth.

"Come," Ian said. "There's something I want to show you." A secluded alcove behind the coat room he'd found during his initial security sweep of the premises where he'd get her to tell the truth. Time was of the essence. Only something big would get Jaci to duck out of such an important event. Ian's body went on full alert, anticipating trouble.

"But I need to—" She tried to pull her hand out of his.

Not a chance, sister. "I've been waiting all night to get you alone," he whispered into her ear as he guided her through the back hallway to their destination. "Ah. Here we are." He dragged her into the dark room, kicked the door closed, and pushed her up against the wall.

"Is there something you want to tell me?" he asked.

Silence.

He started kissing the side of her neck.

She let out a breath and trembled.

Hell, she even responded and tasted like Jaci. Ian's blood started to simmer. How far would she take this charade?

He placed his hands at the curve of her waist. *Stop*

me. Moved them up to her ribs. *Stop me*. An inch more and his thumbs would graze the undersides of her breasts. *Stop me*.

"Ian, stop," Jena said, pushing him away.

Finally. He took a step back. "I was wondering how far you'd let things go." Ian remembered where the light switch was and flicked it on. "Does Jaci know you play it a little fast and loose with her reputation?"

Jena sucked in an appalled breath and looked like he'd taken a swing at her. "Is that what Justin told you?"

"Justin? What does he have to do with this? And if you're here pretending to be Jaci, where the hell is the real Jaci?"

Jena turned away. "I have no idea."

"What?"

"She says it's better if I don't know the details."

Ian wanted to hit something. "And you accept that?"

"Jaci can take care of herself." She wrapped her arms around her middle and looked up at him. "She's been pulling these disappearing acts for years and has never once come across a situation she couldn't handle."

"Oh yeah? Just because she doesn't tell you when she runs into trouble, doesn't mean it's never happened. Take the other night for instance. When Jaci came home all wet."

"She'd done a pick up for the crisis center. It was raining."

"She'd gone down to one of the most dangerous apartment complexes in the county. At night. Alone. And when the girl she was supposed to pick up came out with her boyfriend instead of alone, Jaci confronted them. Thank goodness she'd had the sense to tell her friend to call Justin before leaving her car."

Jena's eyes widened in shock, but Ian didn't stop. He

needed her to understand. "We arrived to find her on the ground in the parking lot. After he'd hit her. At least twice. If we hadn't shown up when we did, he probably would have backed right over her. Or worse."

Urgent male voices sounded in the hallway seconds before the door to their hideaway was thrust open. "She's in here," a man Ian recognized as working security with him and Justin said.

Damn. On break and something had happened. "What's going on?" Ian asked.

A tall, slender, man, late fifties, early sixties, with white hair, a perfectly fitted, top-of-the-line tux, and an air of elitist power about him stepped into the doorway. "Thank goodness," he said, his eyes zeroing in on Jena. "Which one are you?"

"Jaci," Jena answered without hesitation. "What can I do for you Mr. Parks?"

"Millicent has gone missing. You and she were seen discussing what appeared to be a very serious matter earlier, and I wonder if she made mention of some crisis I'm unaware of? A sick friend? An urgent need to be somewhere, perhaps?"

Ian didn't like him. His polished, calm words couldn't hide his barely repressed rage from Ian's trained observer. This man, whose entire demeanor flashed danger, suspected Jaci was involved. God help her. Ian had come in contact with many a man like him. Cool. Calculating. Heartless. Without conscience.

Jena made a seamless transition into the role of Jaci. "Mr. Parks. How terrible." She brought her palm to her cheek. "I'm sure you've checked the ladies room. What can I do to help?"

He stepped closer to her. "You can tell me the topic of your earlier conversation." He stared down, his eyes studying her for any hint of reaction. "That would be helpful."

"It's a private matter, I'd rather not—"

"Damn it, Jaci," he snapped. "This is important." He leaned in close and threatened, "If I find out you had anything to do with this…"

Ian stepped between them.

"Of course I had nothing to do with Millicent's disappearance. My goodness." Jena clutched her chest in a convincing mix of insulted outrage. "The thought! If you must know, we spoke about Jena," Jena said. "Mom and Aunt Mill were so close."

"You know I don't like when you and your sister call her that." His narrowed eyes belied his calm tone, the irises almost glowing with fury.

"She wasn't really our aunt," Jena explained to Ian, and when she looked up at him he saw that she knew Mr. Parks didn't like it. She was playing with him. Very daring. Very Jaci. "Anyway," she turned her attention back to Mr. Parks. "Jena's asked us to keep it quiet, since she has yet to reveal who the father is, but she's the mother of a set of adorable twins. I think I have a picture." She fumbled with her slim purse.

The tip of Mr. Parks's ears turned bright red. "I'm in a bit of a hurry, Jaci. Must you always chatter on? Millicent could be hurt or in the hands of nefarious kidnappers."

Not likely.

"Right. Sorry. I knew Aunt…I mean Millicent would want to know. So I swore her to secrecy, and I told her. Just like that. I couldn't stop myself. Jena will be furious if she finds out so I hope you won't say anything."

A white ring formed where Mr. Parks's lips should be.

"After that, we got to talking about mom, and how

she'd have loved being a grandmother, and how much we both missed her." She wiped at the corner of her eye with her finger.

Damn she was good.

"Where is your sister?" he asked.

"Jena left with a headache about half an hour ago."

"She always was the weaker of the two of you."

Jena didn't react to the barb. "If you must know," she leaned in, "I think it was more new mother anxiety at being separated from her babies."

"Do you think Millicent could have gone to see her?" Mr. Parks asked. He seemed to relax a bit. "That sounds like something she'd do. I bet she couldn't wait until morning."

An apparent pro at subterfuge, Jena said, "Let me call the condo and check." She reached into the bodice of her, well, Jaci's dress, and took out her phone.

He would have gone into battle with this woman in a heartbeat. She and Jaci were made of sturdy stuff.

After speaking on the phone, Jena said, "That was the babysitter. Seems Jena really did have a headache and went right to bed. She's concerned over how pale Jena looked so she's sticking around until I get home. She will be sure to call me if Millicent shows up. If you'll give me your cell number I'll relay the message as soon as I receive it." Jena programed Mr. Parks's number into her phone.

"Let me give you mine, too." Ian took the opportunity to give her his number, just in case.

"She'd have needed a ride. My soon-to-be ex chauffeur isn't answering his phone. He will never get work in this county again." Apparently finished with them, Mr. Parks stormed away.

Jena sagged against the wall and clutched her belly. "I think I'm going to be sick," she whispered.

"You were perfect. You almost had me convinced," Ian said quietly.

"Do you think Jaci had anything to do with Millicent's disappearance?" she whispered.

He thought it a highly unlikely coincidence the two of them went missing at the same time. "I don't know."

"He's mean," Jena said, rubbing her hands together as if to warm them, her face showing the first signs of concern. "Even Jerald gets nervous around him. He is not a man you want to cross."

Yeah, Ian had picked up on that vibe, as well.

"What do we do now?" Jena asked.

"You go out there and be Jaci. Your performance for the next hour or two is the only thing keeping your sister above suspicion." And just barely. "And I go back to work so there is no sign of anything amiss." While he figured out what to do next.

"I can do it," Jena said. "When I'm Jaci, I can do anything."

She was a lot tougher than she gave herself credit. "When this is over you and I need to have a talk about why you think Justin might have told me you play fast and loose with Jaci's reputation."

As poised as she'd been with Mr. Parks, some of Jena's composure slipped at the mention of Justin, for the third time that night. "Is there something going on between the two of you?"

"How could there be?" She took sudden interest in a damaged vase in the corner. "I've been out of town for months."

"*Was* there?"

Sad eyes met his. "Once. But he doesn't want me."

And then it hit him. She hadn't revealed the identity of the father of her babies. It was someone she cared about, and she and Jaci had known Justin since high school. And once was all it took. "Is Justin the father of your twins?"

She looked away, let out a breath, and gave a slight nod.

"Does he know?"

She shook her head, no.

"Does Jaci know?"

She shook her head again, still not looking at him.

"You have to tell him, Jena." Justin would surely do the right thing and marry her.

Jena inhaled then exhaled, stood tall and held her head high. The regal socialite. "I can't talk about this right now. I've got to get out there and be Jaci. Tomorrow I'll return to being boring old Jena and I can resume worrying about how she'll fix the mess she's made of her life."

The real Jaci returned home at three-twenty-six. Three hours and twenty-six minutes later than she'd told Jena to expect her. Three hours and twenty-six minutes during which Ian paced and worried and waited impotently since she'd turned off her cell phone and he'd had no idea what she'd been driving or in what direction she'd been headed. Three hours and twenty-six minutes during which the horrors of the war in Iraq did not intrude on his thoughts once. Because he was too riled up to think about anything other than Jaci and all the possible outcomes of the outrageously stupid stunt he was pretty sure she'd pulled.

In the darkness of Jaci's living room, from the clear view of her sofa, Ian sat, unmoving, his arms crossed over his chest, his hands clenched so tight his nails dug into his palms, watching her slip off her shoes by the door. She tossed a bag onto the counter and the black hair from her wig spilled out.

"You're late," Ian snapped immediately losing the battle to stay in control. "Where the hell have you been?"

She jumped, but recovered quickly. "Gee, Dad, sorry I missed curfew again." She walked into the kitchen. "After the movie, Timmy and I drove down to the lake and stumbled upon a huge keg party." She took a glass from the cabinet and filled it with water. "It was either underage drinking or unprotected sex in the backseat of Timmy's dad's car." She took a sip. "True, the sex would have been a lot quicker, but since you so helpfully pointed out how reckless and irresponsible I always am, I chose the beer figuring it was the less risky of the two. And you know me when I get to talking."

"Cut the crap." He extended and flexed his stiff leg, preparing to stand.

"Go home, Ian," she said, placing her glass in the sink. "None of this is your concern."

Not his concern? When the thought of Jaci getting caught by Parks, or brought to him by one of the many men he no doubt had searching for his wife, filled Ian with a level of fear he'd never experienced, even prior to his most dangerous missions? When the thought of her in danger, or something bad happening to her, or of him losing her made his heart feel like someone had taken a belt sander to it? Pressure started to build in his head. He practically leaped from the couch and pounded toward the kitchen. "Do you have any idea what you've gotten yourself into?"

"Keep your voice down," she whispered. "If you

wake the twins, you're the one who will have to get them back to sleep."

"Do you have any idea what you've gotten yourself into?" he whispered. A whisper didn't do near enough to purge his anger. His pulse pounded. His face felt flush. If Ian didn't unload he'd explode.

"No, Ian. I don't." She looked up at him sweetly. "Perhaps if you speak very slowly and use small words while you explain to me what has you so upset, my addled female brain will be able to process it."

She had the nerve to taunt him? After the hellish past few hours she'd put him through? When he was trying to make her understand she'd made an enemy of a dangerous man? When all he wanted to do was to protect her? From herself as much as from anyone who would want to harm her. He ground his teeth together so tightly it made his jaw ache. He inhaled. Exhaled. Ten. Nine. "Parks cornered Jena."

"No," Jaci said calmly. "Parks cornered Jaci. Jena was home with a headache."

Did she not get it? "He is not someone you want to tangle with," Ian cautioned.

"I have no intention of tangling with him. Other than a nice thank you note for his generous contribution to the center, I don't plan on having any further contact with him."

Like that would deter a man like Parks. "He'll probably get in touch with you." In a dark, deserted place. To threaten and interrogate and do unspeakable things to get the answers he sought. Now all Ian had to do was figure out a way to be with her every minute of every day to make sure the man wasn't given the opportunity to find her alone.

"Whatever for?" she asked innocently.

Ian's eyes felt about ready to shoot from his head. "Maybe because you absconded with his wife," he whispered as forcefully as he could. An intense, violent rage surged inside of him, demanded an outlet, which turned out to be his fist, propelled with the greatest amount of force he could muster, into the side of the cabinet less than a foot from Jaci's head. God help him the release was exactly what he'd needed, the sharp, throbbing pain, exactly what he deserved.

She didn't flinch or move at all just stood there staring at him and said, "You missed."

He didn't miss. He'd hit what he'd been aiming for. The cabinet.

"I should have known it was only a matter of time before you'd take a swing at me, too," she said, no longer whispering.

Too? Ian felt sick.

"Daddy, big strong man that he was, liked to grab me and squeeze while I fought to escape. If I did he'd catch me by the hair, yank me to the ground, and kick me." She pushed Ian's chest to provoke him.

He deserved a hell of a lot more than that. What was wrong with him? Not once in his twenty-eight years had he ever reached the point where he lashed out in anger.

"Come on, Ian. You want to fight?" She pushed him again. "You want to restrain me and dominate me and take all your anger out on me? Sure you do. Because I'm incorrigible and I don't listen and I never do as I'm told. Because I say exactly what's on my mind and I do what I want to do and I refuse to give over control of my life to anyone." She pushed him harder.

He braced the back of his bad leg against the lower kitchen cabinets and kept his hands at his sides prepared to take whatever she planned to dish out.

"That's what men want to do," she said. "Control me. Control my money. What? Nothing to say, tough guy?" She smacked herself in the side of the head. "Then hit me. Get it all out. Jerry likes open-handed smacks to the side of my head. No visible bruising. It'll be our little secret."

Some unnamed emotion squeezed his heart and constricted his lungs, same as when Jaci had recounted the story of her dislocated shoulder at the hands of her father. To think such a kind-hearted, beautiful, delicate woman had been the victim of violence, just like the women she worked so tirelessly to protect. Because no one had been there to protect *her*.

Well that changed today. Ian looked forward to meeting up with Jerry to see how he liked being on the receiving end of an open-handed smack to the head—Ian style.

"Jaci…" His brain failed him, could not come up with the words necessary to convey just how sorry he was, how ashamed and utterly horrified he was by his behavior.

"Wow. Is that remorse I hear in your voice?" She eyed him like the pathetic loser he was. "That's not at all what I expected. Tell me how frustrating I am." She pushed him. "Tell me I'm nice to look at and fun to screw but no man could ever love a woman like me." Tears pooled in her beautiful eyes. "Say the words, Ian. You won't hurt my feelings. I want to hear them."

He said nothing, because the hurt in her expression devastated him, because he could easily love a woman like her, and had circumstances been different, had he been free to pursue the future of his choosing, he'd do anything—*anything*—to earn her love in return. To create a life with her and ignite her passion night after night after night.

But his future had been determined for him. By the maker or makers of a roadside bomb.

Tears spilled down her cheeks. Ian wanted to take her into his arms and comfort her. Comfort him. But he was scared to move, didn't trust himself to do the right thing, wasn't exactly sure what action would best represent the 'right thing'.

Probably leaving and letting her get on with her life. A life without him in it. Yet his feet refused to move.

"Thank you." Jaci wiped at her eyes more mad than sad. "For running out on me when I asked you to marry me. Twenty-five million dollars isn't near enough compensation to put up with this crap." She started to walk away.

Ian held out his arm to stop her as the pieces of the earlier conversation between Jaci and her brother and sister fell into place. "That's a term of your trust fund? That's why you asked me to marry you?" Not because she cared for him or loved him or needed him. Well, she needed him all right. But only so she could inherit twenty-five million dollars. Damn if that didn't sting.

She looked up at him. "I know what you're thinking." She slid her hands in the front pockets of her jeans and looked down at her feet. "Yes I asked you to marry me to meet a requirement of my trust fund. But I chose you because I liked you and cared about you. I thought you liked me, too. We fit. And after that night. Well. Wow."

Yeah. Triple wow.

"I'd planned to explain everything to you but you went off and accused me of being one of *those—*" she made air quotations and emphasized the word *those* "—women."

The kind who equate sex with love. "Well you went off first." After he'd laughed and said, "I've driven women to say a lot of things after sex. But that's my first offer of marriage."

"I didn't propose because of great sex." She looked away.

"You said, 'My God that was amazing. Please say you'll marry me.' What kind of proposal is that? What was I supposed to think?"

She looked about to push him again, but didn't. "Well I'm sorry if it wasn't all you'd hoped for," she snapped. "I'll be sure to do a better job with the next guy I ask to marry me."

Uh oh. Anger started to build. Jaci and another man? Acid churned in his gut. Something foul globbed at the back of his throat. He swallowed. *Keep it cool Ice.* "When do you have to be married by?"

"My twenty-fifth birthday." Like the topic completely zapped her of energy, she pulled out a chair and plopped into it. "In three months."

He pulled out the chair across from her and sat down. "That sucks." For so many reasons, one of them being he'd just taken a swing in her general direction. Not a highly effective prelude into offering oneself up as a husband, he would imagine. And why was that the first thing to pop into his head when he couldn't marry her anyway?

She let out a small laugh. "Especially for someone as difficult as me."

"I meant what I said to your brother," Ian said, trying to catch her gaze. "Any man would be honored to marry you because you're sweet and caring, beautiful and smart, hard-working and dedicated."

"To clarify," she looked him in the eye. "You said any

man with half a brain. What about the ones with fully functioning brains? They'd be too smart?"

Ian shook his head. "You could try the patience of a saint." But he laughed. Because that was Jaci. A whole lot of good and fun with some difficult mixed in to keep things interesting.

"If we hadn't gotten into a fight," she said seriously. "If I'd asked in a different way. What would you have said?"

She would have to ask him that. He entwined his fingers and set his hands on the table. "Honestly? I don't know."

"See," she joked. "Fully functioning brain and you'd have wanted no part of me."

He couldn't hold back a grin.

"Fine," she conceded because she really did seem to always know what he was thinking. "You wanted some parts of me, but not all of me."

Tell me I'm nice to look at and fun to screw but no man could ever love a woman like me. "Things were different then," he explained. "I figured I'd be in the army another ten or twenty years. When I was growing up, my mother despised being married to a man in the military. She hated moving around and being alone with us kids for months at a time then dad coming home and interfering with our routine. I vowed I'd never put a woman through that." Or have to deal with one using love as manipulation, showering him with it or withholding it to get him to do what she wanted then cutting him from her life with the ease of a saber slicing through a banana mid-air when she didn't approve of his decisions. Like his mother had.

"I'm very independent, Ian. I could have handled it."

But he hadn't taken the time to notice or consider

that. And now it was too late. "What are you going to do?" he asked, dreading her response because knowing Jaci, she most likely had something in the works.

She ran a gentle finger over his red knuckles. "My standard answer is 'I won't be forced into marriage'."

He liked that answer.

"But I don't know." She turned in her chair, rested her back against the wall and stretched out her legs. "Twenty-five million dollars could do a lot of people a lot of good." With a shrug she added, "I guess it will go to charity either way."

"That money should go to you. You deserve it." After all she'd been through, she'd earned it. "You should get to decide how it's spent."

"In a perfect world," Jaci mumbled.

"Promise me you won't rush into anything."

She didn't respond, just sat there staring at her feet.

Before he could stop them, the words, "And if, in three months, you haven't found a man you *want* to marry, I'll marry you," tumbled out of his mouth. And you know what?

Although he had no idea how he'd pull off a marriage and meet his commitments to four other families that lived two hours away, he didn't regret them.

"Ah, yes." She stood. "All it took was twenty-five million dollars to make Mr. Why-the-Hell-Would-I-Want-to-Get-Married want to get married."

She threw his words back at him. The money didn't even make his list of top twenty things he found most appealing about Jaci. "I'll sign a prenuptial agreement." He didn't want or need her money. He'd work as many jobs as necessary to meet his financial obligations on his own.

She seemed to consider it…for all of five seconds

then shook her head. "It'll never work. I don't appreciate being reprimanded and interrogated like a child." She crossed her arms over her chest and glared at him.

He stood, crossed his arms over his chest and glared right back. "Then stop sneaking around and taking unnecessary risks like one."

Stalemate.

"*You* chose me, remember?" he pointed out.

"Well things have changed."

Of course. "My leg."

She jerked her head in his direction. "Don't be ridiculous. *You've* changed. You've become moody and bossy and overbearing." She averted her eyes. "And aggressive," she added quietly.

Ian let out a breath. "I'm sorry for that display," he said. "I lost control. Yes. But I aimed for the cabinet. I need you to know you are totally, one hundred percent safe with me. Always. I would never, ever hit you, Jaci. I'm…going through a bit of a rough patch."

Her stubborn expression softened. "P.T.S.D.?" she asked.

He nodded, relieved to finally have it out there and to see understanding and compassion in her beautiful blue eyes.

"You taking your medication as prescribed? Because if you are you need your dosages adjusted." She ended on a sarcastic note.

"I'm not taking any meds." He'd refused, didn't want to spend his days in a state of zombie, dependent on mood altering drugs. He needed to take back control on his own.

"In therapy?" she asked.

He rubbed the side of his head and let out a breath. "After tonight I think I may need to start up again."

She gave him a small smile accompanied by a set of raised eyebrows and a head tilt. "Ya think?"

"I'll call my therapist from rehab for a referral first thing Monday morning."

"Good decision."

"Then you'll consider it? Marrying me?"

"If I can't find anyone else," she clarified, studying him. "You're okay with being the husband of last resort?"

Since he had no intention of letting her marry anyone else, "Sure."

"Maybe you'd better investigate all the particulars before you offer to sacrifice your freedom so willingly." She walked to the oven, picked up the dishtowel hanging over the handle, and wiped down the immaculate counter, placing her back to him. "We'd have to stay married for at least five years."

His first thought: Five years wasn't near long enough. "I'll find a way to work it out." To be there for the wives and children of his men while eking out some happiness and contentment for himself. As long as Jaci agreed to share his time with four other women. Which would have to be addressed at some point. But not tonight.

She turned to face him with a smirk. "Not quite the level of enthusiasm I'd hoped for in a potential if-I-can't-find-anyone-else suitor."

"You want enthusiasm?" he asked, backing her into the counter and pressing his body to hers. "Take me to bed," he whispered in her ear. "And I'll show you enthusiasm."

While he waited for her to accept his offer, a renewed sense of excitement and hope circulated through his system. Maybe he wouldn't have to give up his future after all.

She looked up at him. "No promises." She stepped away and held out her hand palm up. "But I'll consider your offer. And if you're okay with us having sex while I figure out what I'm going to do, let's go."

Ian took the hand she offered and used it to drag her to her bed.

CHAPTER EIGHT

As TIRED as she was after what'd turned out to be a five hour roundtrip drive to drop Millicent Parks at a rest stop on the Thruway, where she met a nameless, faceless contact who would transport her on the next leg of her journey to begin a new life—outside the reach of her well-connected husband, Jaci experienced a resurgence of energy while being hauled down the hall by Ian.

It'd been difficult to say goodbye to Aunt Mill, one of the few positive constants in her and Jena's lives since childhood. Jaci welcomed the opportunity to cleanse her mind of sadness over yet another loss. To replace the eruption of remorse over not doing more to help her mother that occurred each time she facilitated a wealthy woman's escape from her powerful husband, with a state of sex-induced, mind-erasing euphoria that Ian had proven so proficient in providing.

He pulled her into the bedroom, closed the door behind them, and opened his mouth to speak. Jaci reached a finger up to touch his lips. "No talking," she said. She didn't want to explain where she'd been or why she'd arrived home later than expected. She didn't want to discuss Millicent or Mr. Parks, the benefit or her family, marriage or her future or the dozens/hundreds/thousands of women—the ones currently making use of her crisis center's services and the ones she had yet to meet—who were or would one day be dependent on her for a better life.

Tonight Jaci wanted only to feel. The heat of Ian's large naked body pressed to hers. The completeness when he filled that empty place inside of her. The satisfaction of being wanted. The safety of his strong arms. The illusion of being cared for. Loved.

Jaci lifted the bottom hem of his shirt and Ian pulled it up and over his head. She flicked on the light. "I need to see you." His chest wide, the muscles defined, his nipples too tempting to resist.

"I thought you said no talking." He caressed her head as she teased his right nipple with her tongue.

"*You* no talking." She licked a path to the other one. "I can say whatever I want."

Without argument—or another word—he removed her shirt and bra, lifted her to his mouth, and did indeed demonstrate considerable enthusiasm in welcoming her bare breasts to the party. She wrapped her legs around his waist and her arms around his neck. Five years of this would be A.O.K., if not for all the other stuff that'd shifted him from lone occupant on the Definite Marriage Possibility list to the ever growing You'd Kill Each Other in Under a Month list.

This wasn't working. Too much thinking. Not enough doing. Jaci loosened her legs and let them fall from his hips. Not that it mattered since he was plenty strong enough to hold her up without assistance. "I want down," Jaci said. Ian slid her slowly in the direction she sought, maintaining her breasts in full contact with his chest, until her feet touched the floor.

En route, Jaci slipped her finger below the waistband of his jeans and popped the button. He wasn't the only one adept at disrobing the opposite sex one handed. But when she started to lower the zipper he stopped her with his big hand over hers. "Let me get the light," he said.

Because he didn't want her to see his leg. True, it would be easiest to let him plunge the room in darkness so they could fall onto the bed and make some headway in her pursuit of the rapture she craved, without delay. But that wouldn't help Ian come to terms with his injured leg, or show him she accepted his body, as is, and he could feel completely comfortable dropping his pants in her presence.

She tried to maneuver her hand beneath his grip. A futile endeavor.

He held her firm, stood unmoving. Determined.

Well, Jaci had a pretty strong determined streak of her own. And since she routinely found herself at a significant disadvantage strength-wise, she dipped into the bag of womanly attributes she so frequently accessed to get her way and chose cunning. "Make you a deal," she said, then kissed his chest, set her chin on a soft tuft of hair, and looked up at him. "You give me ten minutes of unrestricted access to your body, to do anything I want, and I'll grant you the same in return."

That got his attention.

A risky proposition, yes, because a lot could happen in ten minutes. But it would be well worth it if, in the end, she achieved two desired outcomes. One: Ian realized the sight of his fully naked body would not disgust her or send her running from the room. Two: Ian felt more at ease with the changes to his physique. For that she'd gladly sacrifice a few minutes of the control she'd fought so long and hard to gain.

"I get ten full minutes," he clarified. Jaci could almost feel the vibration of his frenzied plotting regarding how to best make use of those minutes, his mind scrolling through dozens, heck, this was Ian, hundreds of sexual scenarios. Arousal flooded her system in excited anticipation of which one he'd choose. "No matter what," he said. "You run out of here, I drag you back, shut the light, and still get my full ten minutes."

"I'm a nurse, Ian. I have yet to come in contact with a wound or injury I couldn't handle."

Decision apparently made, he moved her hands away and unzipped his pants, exposing a giant erection straining the white cotton fabric of his briefs. Jaci's mouth watered. No reason the unveiling couldn't be enjoyable for both of them. She went down on her knees at his feet, pulled back the elastic waistband and licked the tip, tasted the heady essence of his arousal, and instantly craved more. She slid his underwear and jeans down over his butt, exposing the full magnificence of his manhood, standing thick, and tall and proud like him.

Jaci palmed the base, adjusted the angle, and took him into her mouth. She swirled her tongue, reveled in his taste and the feel of his soft yet firm skin sliding in and out, before she swallowed him deep.

Ian worked his fingers through her hair to her scalp and let out a deep moan.

A wonderfully erotic sound.

Jaci squeezed a butt cheek in each hand and urged him forward, again. When he moved she used his preoccupation to lower his pants to mid-thigh. He stiffened. She resumed focus on his pleasure, cupping him in one hand while moving the other up and down his shaft in tandem with her mouth.

He relaxed.

Until she eased the pants down to his knees and

moved her mouth to hover over his left thigh. "Is it tender to touch?" she asked.

"In some places the skin is hypersensitive. I wouldn't say it hurts, but it feels oddly uncomfortable. In other places I have no sensation at all."

Before casting her gaze down his leg, she kissed his anterior thigh ever so gently and hoped he felt it.

Still on her knees Jaci leaned back. Ian shifted his stance sending his pants to the floor and stood with his hands behind his back. Ready for inspection. Careful to maintain a neutral expression, she began her assessment, immediately understanding why medical personnel were cautioned against treating loved ones in a professional capacity. Where in the course of her work she would evaluate a wound objectively and without emotion, what she saw sent a painful, breath-halting pang through her chest.

This man standing before her wasn't a post-op open reduction internal fixation of the femur or a non-healing ankle ulcer in need of daily dressing changes. He wasn't a patient to be treated with clinical detachment and professional distance—not that she'd ever truly mastered either.

He was Ian. Her friend. A man she cared about and admired, way more than she wanted to admit, way more than was safe for her heart. A man whose lower extremities bore the markings of the significant and horrific physical trauma he'd endured.

Do not cry. Don't you dare cry.

Two legs, left *and* right, once perfect in form, now ravaged and flawed.

Mentally prepared to see only his left leg disfigured, the sight of deep reddish purplish donor skin graft sites on his right leg took her by complete surprise. A large rectangular area on his inner thigh stretching from groin to knee, one on his outer calf extending from knee to ankle and two smaller rectangular patches horizontally parallel to each other mid-thigh.

The pain must have been excruciating.

As gently as she could, she kissed each one.

"Five minutes," Ian said quietly.

Of course he'd be keeping time. Jaci studied his left leg, letting her eyes travel along a network of healed, zipper-like suture lines of varying shades of pink to red, winding from ankle to upper thigh, around a patchwork of healthy-looking skin grafts. The leg itself was noticeably thinner, with textural irregularities, hypertrophic and widened scarring, and numerous asymmetrical defects. But aside from a few areas of dry, flaky skin, both legs seemed to have healed nicely.

Jaci looked up to see Ian's eyes focused on hers. She stood. "You are standing unassisted on your own two legs. Granted, they're not as pretty as they used to be." He knew the truth as well as she did, so why sugarcoat it. "But a person is more than the condition or sum of his physical parts. What makes you special is what's in here." She reached up to touch his temple. "And what's in here." She placed her other hand over his heart.

"It's finding Maria's boyfriend a job at a local bodega," she said. "Then volunteering your services and your S.U.V. to help them move into the apartment above it." She wrapped her arms around him and pulled him close. "It's going out of your way, despite being in pain, to help me, my patients, their families and neighbors after the worst end-of-summer storm to hit the area in a decade. It's you getting angry and being a total pain in my butt because you're concerned about me."

"Because I care about you," he said, finally hugging her back and kissing the top of her head.

About her body, maybe. "I care about you, too," Jaci admitted. Really cared about him. "But I could do without the overprotective big brother crap."

"Believe me when I tell you," he moved his hands to the button of her slacks. "What I feel for you is not at all big-brotherly." By the time the words were out he was sliding her pants and panties down her legs. "And shazzam." He sounded back to his old self. "Your time is up and mine has begun."

"I may need a few minutes—" he bent down and kissed her before she could share the most important part of that sentence "—to get back in the mood." Unlike him, the heavy emotional toll of the past few minutes— He scooped her up and carried her to the bed, lay down on top of her and deepened the kiss. His lips smooth, his tongue plunging into her mouth while a hand fondled her breast and his thigh settled between her legs. And well what'd'ya know? Just like that she was back in the game.

He lifted his head just enough for their eyes to connect. "Do you trust me?" he asked.

An innocuous enough question, if not for the fact they were naked, and the need for trust most likely indicated an excursion outside usual and customary bed play. Four words she didn't hear often in her current situation, and when she did, four words to which she always responded, "No."

But she did trust Ian and believed she was safe with him. And she *had* promised him ten unrestricted minutes. So, "Yes." She tried to glance at the clock to see a start time, just in case, but a pillow rested on top of it. Had he done that on purpose? "Hey, I—"

He jumped off the bed so abruptly and turned her so quickly it robbed Jaci of speech. Then he pulled her to the edge until her head fell backwards over the side.

Standing over her, his legs slightly spread, he looked down and asked, "Comfy?"

Yeah, if she ignored the blood accumulating in her brain. But her upside down view of the underneath side of his male member sparked an interest in just what he had in mind. She nodded. Good man that he was he slid the tip of his erection along the seam of her lips, not making her wait to find out.

"Open up." She did. "If you want me to stop just tap my leg." She nodded. Apprehensive, yet gung ho to try something new. With Ian.

Her position opened her throat and elongated her neck—her airway—and Jaci understood why she would need to trust him. He started off slow, filling her mouth, pulling all the way out then slowly sliding in again and again. Jaci upped the ante lifting her head to meet him, her lips, cheeks, and tongue active participants.

He groaned. "This is one instance when reality is so much better than fantasy." He thrust deep, tapped at the back of her throat, held completely still.

Jaci didn't panic, knew he wouldn't leave her without air for long. In truth she liked this test, this reminder that she had full confidence in Ian as a lover.

He pulled out, breathing heavy. "Bend your legs."

She did. He leaned over her body, grabbed her behind each knee, and draped one leg then the other over the backs of his elbows. In the process he lifted her butt off the bed, opened her wide, and brought her most private parts a few scant inches from his mouth. Thank goodness she hadn't skimped on the waxing in preparation for last night's event.

"Beautiful." He dipped his knuckle into her opening, twirled in tight little circles, then distributed her wetness front to back. There. An area that, until that very minute, had never been touched by male hands. Or any other part of the male anatomy for that matter. Whoa.

"Relax," he encouraged.

Easy for him to say. He knew exactly what he had planned. She didn't. "What time is it?"

He answered by setting his mouth on her oh-yeah-right-there spot and erased all thoughts unrelated to the pursuit of pleasure from her head. Arousal pulsed through her veins. A finger, two, no three, plunged deep inside of her. Over and over. And another. Testing. A delicious pressure, absolutely sublime. "That's so good." She rocked her hips. Wanting more. He gave it to her. So close. But Jaci didn't want to come alone.

She reached up and brought Ian's erection down to her mouth. Upon contact he took over. Filling her. Everywhere. Driving into her, taking her higher, ratcheting up the intensity.

And then, with no warning, he pulled out. Abandoned her.

"No!" She'd been so close.

He lifted her head gently and rotated her on the bed until her head rested in the middle and her legs fell over the side. He sheathed himself. She bent her legs, setting her feet on the edge of the mattress. Opening for him. Waiting.

"I want to see your face when we make love." He leaned over her and settled his hardness between her legs. "I want to see your pleasure." He drove into her. "Watch your lips pucker and hear the urgency of your little moans." He pulled out and thrust back in. "Watch your eyes roll back in your head when you come."

Jaci wrapped her legs around his hips and watched him right back. The intensity of his gaze, the affection and lust and determination to please her. She listened to his rapid, harsh breaths. The sound of skin on skin.

Her eyelids tried to drift closed at the feel of him, filling more than her physical form. He felt right. Like this was meant to be. Perfection.

And as body and soul surrendered to Ian, Jaci remained cognizant just long enough to enjoy Ian's climax and feel the collapse of his heavy weight on top of her, before she allowed herself to swirl off into a sea of spectacularness.

"I haven't seen you smile this much since we opened our doors," Carla said, coming to stand beside Jaci.

Superb loving did that to a woman. Every night for the past six nights. "Life is good." She smiled as she watched Ian play Slap Jack with two of the older boys who resided at the center with their mothers. He was an excellent role model, and after school the boys basically shadowed him everywhere.

"I have to admit I had my concerns about bringing a man on staff," Carla said. "But in his first week on the job, Ian's managed to win over everyone. Even Monique."

They both watched as tiny, painfully thin Monique, who spoke only when spoken to and rarely lifted her eyes from the floor, carried two coffee mugs to the farthest empty table in the common room and sat down. Then Ian excused himself from his card game—to groans of unhappiness, stood, and joined Monique. The two spoke quietly.

"What's that all about?" Jaci asked.

"Ian told me someone informed him, confidentially,

that Monique had been receiving threatening messages from her husband. Ian asked if it was okay for him to try to get her to talk to him about it. I told him to go ahead."

To date Monique had not said one word in her group or private therapy sessions, and she'd been an onsite resident for over two months. Yet there she sat, huddled next to Ian, talking quietly. She handed him her cellphone.

"Your man has a genuine gift," Carla said.

He truly did. Jaci was about to say, "He isn't my man." But she kind of liked him being referred to as such. Ian fit into her life better than she'd ever imagined any man would. And based on his actions and how he went about doing his job, arriving early and staying late, in the very short time he'd worked there, the residents of the crisis center had become just as important to him as they were to her.

And so far, other than a minor argument about the cost of the high tech security system Ian wanted to have installed, for which he finally agreed to search out less expensive options, his transition into the new position of head of security and facility maintenance had been without incident.

"Mr. Eddelton?"

Ian retrieved the file on bids for a new security system, closed the file drawer, and returned to his desk. He leaned forward to depress the intercom button on his phone. "Yes, Andrea?" He tried not to sound curt, but the time he'd spent with the boys and Monique put him behind on the report he'd told Jaci he would have on her desk first thing Monday morning. And after the call he'd received from The Kid's wife this afternoon, he wouldn't be around this weekend to finish it up on his days off.

"Remember how you told me if anyone entering the lobby makes me even a little bit nervous I should contact you right away?" the receptionist asked quietly.

Ian went on alert. "Yes."

"And remember how you told me that even if Ms. Piermont tells me not to bother you I should still tell you and you'll make sure she doesn't fire me?"

Come on. "Yes, Andrea. I remember." Get to the point.

"A few minutes ago an older man came in asking for Ms. Piermont. I told him she was in with a patient but he started yelling and said he'd take this place apart brick by brick—" Ian ran to Jaci's office.

Empty.

Carla's office.

Empty.

To the large common area, where he saw Jaci talking amicably with a somewhat tousled and less put together version of the Mr. Parks he'd met at the benefit.

Frankly, Ian had expected him much sooner. Anger started to build. Why the heck hadn't Jaci informed him of Mr. Parks's visit? And why was she walking with him toward the private, staff only area of the building which would be deserted this late on a Friday afternoon?

An image of Mr. Parks standing over Jaci, his hands around her throat, squeezing the life from her while he questioned her about his wife's whereabouts flashed.

Ian shifted into battle ready and headed toward them.

"Why didn't you tell me we had a visitor?" he asked in his most congenial tone when he reached Jaci.

"Because I didn't want you to make a big deal of Mr. Parks's friendly visit," Jaci replied with a smile. "He is a very generous benefactor of the Women's Crisis Center and, of course, is welcome to stop in for a tour any time he's in the area."

Regardless of what brought him to the area or his intentions while on site? "Hello, Mr. Parks." Ian held out his hand. "Ian Eddelton. We met at the benefit."

Mr. Parks glanced at Ian, shook his hand then returned his attention to scanning his surroundings. His eyes darting to any movement, any sound.

This was no friendly visit. Mr. Parks was on the hunt.

"I'll take it from here," Ian offered. "Shouldn't you be in with the doctor and our new arrival?"

"Don't be ridiculous," Jaci said with another smile. This one forced and accompanied by tightening around her eyes. "I always have time to show off our beautiful facility and brag about the wonderful work we do around here."

She'd shifted into fundraising socialite mode. That's when Ian noticed she'd changed out of the scrubs she'd been wearing earlier and into a set of brown pleated slacks, pointy toed brown heels, and a short-sleeved, cream-colored, cashmere sweater.

Well friendly visit or not, Ian wanted Jaci far away from Mr. Parks. Every moment they spent in each other's company increased the risk she'd slip up and Mr. Parks would identify some inconsistency that would further fuel his suspicions of Jaci's involvement in the disappearance of his wife. And make him more aggressive in his search for answers.

Jaci hadn't seen the accusation and distrust in the man's eyes or heard the threatening warning in his tone when Mr. Parks had confronted Jena thinking she was Jaci. *If I find out you had anything to do with this...*

"I'll take good care of Mr. Parks." Ian put his hands

on her shoulders and turned her in the direction of her office.

She continued around to face him. "Stop it." She glared up at him. "I'll be the one giving Mr. Parks his tour."

"Would you excuse us for a moment?" Ian asked Mr. Parks, and, not waiting for an answer, he pulled Jaci out of ears reach. "I will handle Mr. Parks," Ian said. "Go to your office and wait for me there."

"Absolutely not," she snapped in a whisper. "You are creating an unnecessary scene."

"Which I will stop when you leave."

Jaci looked on the verge of a major blowup.

"You will not win." He stared her into silence. "Go. Now."

She walked over to Mr. Parks and took his hand. "Ian just reminded me of an urgent matter I need to attend to. And he's graciously offered to give you a tour." Then she whipped around—lucky for him her eyes weren't loaded or he'd have a bullet lodged between his eyes—and stormed off.

So she was mad. At least she was safe.

The tour took just under forty-five minutes and, at Mr. Parks's insistence, included the electrical room, janitorial closet, and basement. "So you see," Ian said to Mr. Parks as he accompanied him back to the lobby. "Your wife isn't here." Ian let him know he knew the real reason for today's visit.

Mr. Parks showed no reaction.

"And before I start to wonder why you thought she might be hiding in a crisis center that houses women who have been displaced as the result of abusive relationships, you'd better turn the focus of your search away from Jaci."

"I *will* find Millicent," Mr. Parks insisted.

Ian hoped the woman was far away and well hidden. "I wish you the best of luck, sir," he lied.

"And when I do—"

"You will owe Jaci an apology." They reached the door to the lobby. Ian turned to block Mr. Parks's path. "Your suspicion of Jaci stops today." Ian stared the villain down. "You stay away from her."

He didn't react to Ian's look or tone of menace that typically sent seasoned soldiers running for cover.

Ian opened the door and Mr. Parks walked through it. Good riddance.

But he knew better than to believe that was the end.

"You should have let Jaci handle him," Carla said from behind him. "She wants to see you in her office."

Well he wanted to see her, too. What the hell was she thinking sneaking Parks into the center without telling him? Ian broke out in a cold sweat at the thought of Jaci alone with that man in the dank, poorly lit basement.

He found her door open, per usual, with Jaci sitting behind her desk. When she saw him, she hit a button on her computer and her printer clicked into action. "Come in and close the door." She stood. All business.

As soon as they were alone she let him have it. "How dare you send me to my office like a parent banishing a child to their room?" *He'd done nothing of the sort.* "How dare you usurp my position here and mitigate my authority by ignoring me when I told you I would be the one giving Mr. Parks his tour?" *That had nothing to do with her position or authority and everything to do with keeping her out of harm's reach. And Ian would do it again in a heartbeat.* "Do not for one minute forget who you report to." She snatched a piece of paper off the printer and handed it to him. "Read this, and sign it."

He looked down and scanned the words.

The heading: Employee Disciplinary Action Form.

His body went rigid.

Type of Violation: The box for Disobedience had a capital, bold-faced X in it.

Violation? Disobedience? While he'd accompanied their 'guest' on a tour of the bowels of the building, Jaci had embarked on her own excursion. Of the power trip variety.

Employer Statement: Head of Security failed to acknowledge and respect an upper level manager's statement then proceeded to act in a heavy-handed and intimidating manner.

Intimidating his ass. Nothing intimidated Jaci.

Warning Decision: Further infraction of the managerial hierarchy will result in immediate termination.

A heated anger frothed up from his core. Termination? He jammed his left hand into his pants pocket so she couldn't see the tight fist his fingers had curled into. She was just like his mother and sisters. He didn't act the way she wanted or do things according to her plan and she wanted to get rid of him. Boom. Done.

"Are you kidding me? All I did was protect you from a dangerous man who has it in for you. And you're threatening me with termination?" On his fifth full day of work? Ian had never in his life, since he'd gotten his first job at the age of fourteen, been disciplined by an employer or threatened with termination/discharge. If anything, he'd been commended for exemplary commitment and performance. He had the commendation medals for distinguished service to prove it.

"You are home from the war, Ian," she said calmly. "Not everyone poses a threat. By inserting yourself into the situation with Mr. Parks, by not letting me handle him on my own, you made it appear I have something to hide."

"You do," he yelled. This was absurd. He took a step toward her, wanted to shake some sense into her. "Did you know Parks called off the official search for his wife?"

She stepped away from him. From her surprised expression, no she didn't.

"I asked Justin to make a few discreet inquiries. Apparently he contacted the police a few hours after leaving the benefit to say he'd returned home to find a note from his wife saying she'd gone to visit her sister. Based on his visit here, he's taken it upon himself to continue the search on his own terms. By his own rules." Which meant no rules.

Jaci glared up at him. "You underestimate me if you think I'm incapable of handling a man like Mr. Parks." She unlocked a drawer of her desk. "I have lived my life surrounded by pompous, self-important, power-hungry clones of him. I can walk the walk and talk the talk with the best of them." She held up two sealed envelopes.

As part of his orientation he'd been shown the locked file cabinet where Jaci and Carla maintained pictorial documentation of the injuries inflicted on their clients by their abusers. "You have pictures?"

She slammed one envelope on her desk. "A letter from his wife telling him to stop his search or she would expose him for tax evasion. Which, now that he has demonstrated an interest in me as an accomplice, I will mail to a contact in Texas tomorrow and she will mail to Mr. Parks upon receipt."

She slammed a second envelope on her desk. "A letter of explanation and a key to a safety deposit box that contains the documentation necessary to send Mr. Parks to prison. He comes here again or I feel threatened in any way, I mail it to the district attorney's office. Anything happens to me, Carla hand delivers it."

Waiting until after something happened to her was not an option.

"And for your information, Ian, not all abuse is physical. Emotional abuse is a pattern of behavior aimed at insulting, humiliating, degrading, threatening, isolating and/or *controlling* another person."

She placed special emphasis on the word 'controlling' and aimed it directly at him. "Even when you're exerting that control in the other person's best interest?" he asked. Because she chose not to acknowledge the inherent danger in dealing with the seedy underbelly of society—Mr. Parks included—or maintain a healthy fear of it?

"You don't get to decide what's in my best interest," she snapped. "Just like Mr. Parks does not get to decide what's in Aunt Mill's best interest. We're not children. Why do men feel they have authority over us? That it's their God given right to dominate us and bend us to their will?"

Ian studied her.

"What?" she asked.

"The men in your family really did a number on you." He shook his head.

"What is that supposed to mean?"

"You're so busy fighting against what you perceive as a man's attempt to control you, you're blind to the fact I act the way I do because I care about you, and I'm concerned for your safety."

She looked shell-shocked. Had she never had a man tell her he cared for her before?

"This isn't about me trying to dominate you or manipulate you," he explained. "It's about me trying to protect you. And I can't figure out if you actually believe you're invincible, if you're so overwrought with guilt over what happened to your parents you tempt fate for the chance to join them in the hereafter so you can apologize, or if you're just too naïve to realize when someone poses a threat to you."

"Get out," Jaci screamed and pointed toward the door.

"Gladly." Ian ripped the Employee Disciplinary Action Form down the middle and tossed it on her desk. "If you want me to stay on as head of security, I do my job my way."

She started to say something but he cut her off with a raised hand. "You hired me for my expertise and you need to trust my instincts. Even if you don't like what they're saying. If you can't do that, fire me." With that he turned and left her office.

CHAPTER NINE

"DID I mention I worked today, and I'm exhausted?" Jaci asked, knowing, yes, she had. At least three times. But the investment banker from the tenth floor liked to talk more than he liked to listen. Two more minutes and she'd belt out the truth. "Your cologne makes the back of my nose itch, I don't date men with fingernails longer and better maintained than mine, and you drink scotch, neat, which is a definite deal breaker."

But in deference to his upstairs neighbor status, determined to end on a friendly note, she held off.

He leaned close and Jaci backed up as far as she could, purposely banging her elbow on the door to her condo, hoping Jena would hear and come to investigate.

"I still can't believe *The* Jaci Piermont has an actual job."

The smell of his liquored-up breath, the slight slur in his speech, and the way he boxed her in brought back unwanted memories.

"There's nowhere to run, Jaci."

"Come on, girl, you can do better than that."

"Fight all you want. Daddy's not letting go until you calm down."

"Not so tough now, are you?"

She shook them off. "If I didn't work, how would I spend my days?"

She tried to slip away.

He twirled one of her curls around his freakishly long, thin, almost womanly index finger and held her in place. "Strolling the Avenue des Champs-élysées. Visiting the beaches of Bali. Shopping in Milan. Skiing in Switzerland. Yachting in the Maldives."

For the umpteenth time that night she compared him to Ian, and for the umpteenth time he didn't come close to measuring up. "Look…" Shoot. She'd been referring to him as the investment banker up on ten for so long, that's the only identifier that came to mind. *Think*. Oh, right. Richard. "I'm tired, Richard."

This entire evening had been a mistake, another poorly thought out hastily made decision that'd backfired.

"I told you to call me Dickie."

Not even if he were under the age of three. "Date's over."

"It doesn't have to be."

As far as Jaci was concerned, their date had gone on way longer than it should have, already.

"Ask me in," he whispered.

Not even for twenty-five million dollars. "Maybe another time." Code for never, ever, as long as she lived. Apparently Richard did not like the 'maybe another time' idea, and yet one more reason Brandon at the concierge desk never saw him with the same woman twice became glaringly obvious. Jaci looked up at him. "Remove your hand from my breast this instant or you'll be sorry."

He smiled.

Incorrect response number one.

And squeezed.

Incorrect response number two.

So she hauled off and landed a palm heel strike to Dickie's nose. Newsflash: That mandatory self-defense in-service she'd taken at work a few months ago was no joke. The stunned investment banker from ten jumped back and grabbed his bleeding snout exactly like the instructor had said he would, giving Jaci the chance to unlock her door, utter a quick, "Good night," and hightail it inside.

She let out a relieved breath.

That's it. There would be no marriage. No twenty-five million dollars. No men period. Jaci Piermont was officially off the market.

Someone knocked.

She jumped.

Jena hurried down the hallway. "Open the door. It's Ian."

Ian, who'd stormed out of her office five days ago and had not responded to one of her phone calls since then? Ian, who left overnight messages for the receptionist calling out sick from work for three days with no explanation? Ian, who ran out on her, again, and pissed her off to the point she'd gone out on tonight's god-awful date to prove to herself it didn't matter? That he didn't matter?

Damn if her heart didn't pound out a couple of extra happy beats at the idea of his return. But, "Why would Ian be knocking on our door at," she looked at her watch, "after ten o'clock on a Wednesday night?"

"I called him."

"Why would you call him?" And why did he answer Jena's call and not hers?

"I was watching through the peephole."

"You voyeur," Jaci teased.

Jena shrugged. Unrepentant. "A single mother of twins has to get her kicks somehow."

"So you saw no-longer-a-husband-candidate put the moves on me and thought rather than open the door to bring a halt to the action, you'd call Ian?"

"I didn't want to give that miscreant the opportunity to push inside."

A valid point.

"How did you know he was home?" Since Jaci had been complaining about him being gone since he'd left.

"He called earlier, said he needed to talk to you when you got in."

Another knock. Harder this time. "Open the door, Jaci."

Jena pushed Jaci out of the way and opened the door. And in strolled Ian calm as can be. "Did you know there's a man bleeding outside in the hallway?"

Jena closed the door and pointed at Jaci.

"I wonder what could have happened," Jaci said innocently.

"I think I heard him mumble something about a hell-cat." Ian gave her a stern look. "He's a pale pansy who probably thinks a barbell is something a bartender rings at the start of happy hour. A ten-year-old could have taken him. Don't get overconfident in your abilities."

"Pleasure to have you home," she said dryly. But it was. She'd missed him, worried about him and ached for him. And the date meant to distract her and prove she wasn't crazy in love with Ian had only served to prove the opposite. "Turns out the investment banker as a potential husband candidate was a catastrophic fail."

"Good," Ian said, looking serious.

"I'm off to bed," Jena said and left them.

"*Not* good." Jaci looked up at Ian. "And I hold you," she poked his chest with her index finger, "responsible."

"Ouch." He brought his hand up to the area of assault and rubbed. "Me? What did I do?"

"You're all..." She scanned his tall, muscled body. And, well, YUM. "You're all...you."

"That makes a lot of sense. How much did you have to drink tonight?"

"Trust me, not near enough." Remembering she had half a bottle of wine in the fridge, Jaci walked into the kitchen, grabbed two glasses from the cabinet, and retrieved it. "You want some?" She held it up.

"No." Ian joined her in the kitchen. "And would you mind holding off on getting hammered for a little bit? We need to talk."

His grim tone told Jaci she would not enjoy their 'talk' one bit.

She turned to face him as he pulled a chair out from beneath her small table, sat down and rubbed his hand down his face from forehead to chin. "I don't want to..."

...marry you...work for you...have anything to do with you. Because she was headstrong and difficult and...damaged. Just like he'd said. Because the men in her family had done a number on her. She braced herself for Ian's rejection, knowing it would hurt a thousand times worse than anything her father or stepbrother could dish out.

"...fight with you," he finished.

Huh? That wasn't at all what she'd expected. "I don't want to fight with you, either." She sat down across from him. But she'd spent so many years fighting, she didn't know how to stop.

"We need to get better at talking."

She smiled. "This coming from a man?"

He smiled back. "Ironic. I know." He inhaled and let out a breath. "I may have overreacted to Mr. Parks's visit. I'm sorry." He looked down at his lap. "But I need you to understand where I'm coming from." Silence.

Jaci waited it out.

"In my ten years in the army, fighting for freedom and human rights, I have seen the worst of human nature. Unspeakable atrocities and depravities you can't begin to imagine. They color my thinking and impact my decision making and yes, maybe make me overly cautious." He lifted his head to look at her. "The thought of your beauty, sweetness, and blind compassion being touched by the hand of evil tears me up inside. The fear of it drives me to take action to shield you. It's who I am, Jaci. I protect. I take care of."

Which made him perfect for work at the crisis center, but probably not for a fiercely independent woman with control issues.

"You know I can tell what you're thinking, too," he said.

Busted! "It's just…" Just what? She hated to be told what to do? Childish. Hated that he didn't think her capable of making wise decisions? Better.

"I know," he said without waiting for her to finish. "But if *I* try to back off a bit and learn to trust your judgment and *you* agree to consider 'what would Ian want me to do in this situation' before you act, maybe we can meet up in the middle?"

"That depends," Jaci teased. "After considering what you'd want me to do would I actually have to do what you'd want me to do?"

He nodded. "That's the plan, yes."

"Well I don't see that as meeting in the middle."

"Then why don't we take it a step further." He placed

his elbows on the table and leaned toward her. "What would Ian want me to do in this situation so I can return home to him safe and sound and he can reward me by doing wonderfully erotic things to my body?"

She swallowed, imagining a few 'wonderfully erotic things' she'd like to try. "That works."

Based on the gleam in his eye, he did, in fact, know what she was thinking.

"And about us getting married."

Fun time over. Here it came. The kiss-off…

"I don't want to be your husband of last resort."

Of course he didn't. "Which is fine." She stood. At dinner, while alone at the table awaiting the return of her date, she'd decided to hell with scampering around to find a husband to meet terms dictated by her father. His control over her life ended tonight. "I don't want to be married, anyway." But his statement still hurt. She stretched. "It's been a long—"

"I don't think you're understanding me." He stood, too. "Rather than stand by and hope you don't find another man you want to marry so I get to marry you by default, I'd rather we spend the next few months together, exclusively, really getting to know each other and learning how to live together. If we get married, I want it to be because we're in love and plan to stay together forever."

The fairytale ending she didn't dare dream of ever happening for her. She fought back tears.

"But if you don't want the same thing—"

He mistook her silence.

She lunged at him and hugged him tight. "I do. It's exactly what I want."

He kissed the top of her head. "So no more dates."

As if that needed to be said out loud. She looked up

at him. "You want to know how I spent a good part of my time tonight?"

He eyed her cautiously, his hands clasped at her back. "I'm not sure I want the specifics."

"Comparing my date to you."

A more self-satisfied grin she'd never seen. "I like it."

"Ian wouldn't have humiliated the waitress by carrying on and complaining to the manager over a spilled glass of ice water," she recounted.

He shook his head. "Never."

"Ian wouldn't have been so rude as to answer his phone or excuse himself from the table during dinner, for an extended period of time, to take a call from a business associate," she added. "He would never show a complete disinterest in what I had to say by reading and responding to text messages during our conversations."

"Now that I know a broken nose is the price to pay, you can be sure I won't do it in the future, either."

"Ha. Ha. The nose bit was in response to him putting his hands where they weren't welcome."

He stiffened. Grimaced.

And she kind of liked the display of jealousy. But, "Calm down, big guy." She caressed his upper arms. "You've been doing so well up to now. Sit."

He did. And Jaci positioned herself behind him and began to massage his neck and shoulders.

"I'm back in therapy three times per week and back to working out," he said. "I spent two hours in the gym tonight."

Nothing got her going like Ian all sweaty and manly after a hard workout. Hot. Hot. Hot.

"But there is still work to be done. I'll be honest. If I'd arrived downstairs in time to see that bastard's hands on you, I cannot say with any certainty that I wouldn't have knocked him unconscious."

Strangely enough, Jaci would have been okay with that.

"I'm trying." He sat forward, rested his elbows on the table, and clasped his fingers together.

"You'll get there. I know you will." She hugged him from behind. "In your own time. There's no need to rush. And I'll help in any way I can."

"Regular sex seems to be helping."

"Must be my therapeutic touch." She held out her fingers and wiggled them.

He pulled her onto his lap. "I've missed you."

"I've missed you, too," she admitted, loving the feel of his strong arms wrapped around her. "Which brings me to the question of where did you disappear to? And why didn't you answer my phone calls? I was worried about you." And she had no intention of letting him off the hook for deserting her without a word. Again.

"I'll get to where I was in a minute. Maybe you'd better go back to your seat across from me." He gave her a little push.

Uh oh. She did.

"As far as why I didn't answer your calls, I thought we could both do with some time apart. But I listened to each one of your messages to make sure there weren't any emergencies."

"Let me clue you in," Jaci said. "Women are talkers. We like to know what people are thinking. In the absence of communication, we form our own conclusions. I thought you'd gone for good and we were through."

"Well, *I* thought a little distance would give us both a chance to cool off." His eyes met hers. "You can be sure if I'd even considered the possibility it'd send you off on a date with another man, I would have done things differently."

"It all worked out for the best, though." Jaci shrugged. "My date with Dickie-the-dog reminded me of all the things I don't want in a man." She reached across the table, took his hand between hers, and added, "And all the things I do. Now tell me where you've been so we can go to bed and commence with the makeup sex."

Makeup sex. Ian would be lucky to get any sex after what he'd done. But there was no turning back. He'd gotten Jaci on board with the spending time together, exclusivity, and marrying for love plan. Now to present his marriage deal breaker. Ian swallowed. His entire future hinged on the next few minutes, which he would not rush.

So he started at the beginning.

"The day I turned eighteen I enlisted in the army," he started. "On that same day my mom and sisters cut off all contact with me, said they couldn't go through losing another family member to war, like we'd lost my dad."

"Oh, Ian. I'm sorry."

"I'm over it." Most of the time. "Because the men in my squad took me in and became my family, my brothers. Stateside, I visited them, spent holidays with them and got to know their wives and kids. Overseas, we looked out for each other. They saved my ass on more than one occasion. And I returned the favor every chance I got."

He took a deep breath. This next part was the toughie and odds were pretty much even whether he'd get through it without breaking down. "I lost my four closest friends that last night in Iraq." Kid—the youngest in the group. Mac—MacPhearson. MP—for meat and potatoes, all the man would eat. Lucky—who had the prettiest wife.

The deafening boom of the IED exploded in his ears. He grabbed for them.

His leg. Pain. Burning. Stuck. His body thrashed around the Humvee. Gunfire.

"You guys okay?"

No answer. Another explosion close by. Smoke. Heat. Darkness.

"Guys?"

No response.

"Medic. Medic!"

All alone. All. Alone.

"Hey." Jaci's voice. "You're okay." She moved his hands from his ears.

He didn't feel like he'd ever be okay.

She kissed his temple. "You're not all alone."

Had he said that out loud?

"You have me." She kissed his forehead. "And Justin." She kissed his cheek.

He sucked in a breath. Felt winded.

"You don't have to talk about this if you're not ready." She gave him an out.

He didn't take it. "I need you to understand how much those men meant to me. How much their families mean to me, how I consider them my family."

"Of course you do."

"And in the absence of my brothers, the responsibility for their wives and kids falls to me, the last man standing. They're not here. But I am. To look out for their families like they looked out for me. My brothers." Tears streamed down his cheeks.

Jaci hugged him to her chest and kissed the top of his head.

"I miss them," Ian admitted out loud, for the first time since their deaths. "I miss them so much."

Jaci pushed herself onto his lap and pulled him into a hug.

He dropped his head to her shoulder, hugged her back, so tight. She didn't complain. And Ian cried. For all that he had lost. All that had been taken from him. The unfairness of it. The anger that raged inside of him. Guilt, for having lived…and now, for daring to fall in love. With Jaci. For daring to hope for a happy future when his men had no future and the futures of their wives and children would be forever marred by death and sorrow.

Jaci didn't move. Didn't speak. She just sat there, rubbing his back. For minutes? Hours? He didn't know.

Finally, when he'd released four months of pent up tears Ian whispered, "Thank you."

"I bet you needed that," was all she said.

She had no idea how much. He reached for a napkin to dry his eyes. "On the macho meter I guess I'm ranking a negative ten about now."

"Maybe for some women. But on the Jaci Piermont attraction meter you are into triple-digit sexy."

Right where he wanted to be.

"I'm assuming the death of your men and your responsibility to their families has something to do with where you were for the past five days?" She traced the rim of his ear with her finger.

He nodded. "The Kid's wife has been having a tough time and she asked me to come." Begged and pleaded until he knew he could not put it off any longer. "I'd planned to tell you."

"It's okay," Jaci said. "I understand."

"And I hope you'll also understand how important

these four women and their seven children are to me. And now that I'm able, I'll be visiting them, regularly, probably every weekend."

"We," Jaci said.

He looked at her.

"We'll be visiting them. We'll be helping them out. For as long as we're together, it's we."

Ian's heart swelled with love. "You're not going to tell me I'm crazy? That they're not my responsibility? That I'm acting out of guilt?"

"You're doing what you feel you have to do. And it's the right thing to do. When can I meet them?"

The kicker. He ran his hand behind his neck. "Well… You can meet Mandy, The Kid's wife, as soon as you want." Wait for it. "She and her baby are upstairs in my condo."

After the fit Justin had thrown, Ian could just imagine how Jaci'd react. He didn't dare look at her. "I didn't know what else to do," he explained. "She looks terrible, so pale and thin. I mean she was thin before but now she's sickly thin. The house was a mess. There was hardly any food in the refrigerator. The baby has a terrible diaper rash." At least it looked terrible to him. "She has no family. I couldn't leave her there and I didn't want to stay. So I packed up her condo, hitched a rental trailer to the back of my S.U.V., and brought her home with me." And he had no plan past that.

Jaci slid off his lap.

That's it. He'd lost her.

"How old is the baby?" she asked.

Not exactly the first thing he'd expected to come out of her mouth.

"A little over a year old."

"Are you insane?" she asked.

Here it came. He resisted the urge to squint and turn away when she laid into him for bringing a woman and baby into their lives.

"Leaving a distraught woman and a toddler alone in a strange condo? There's nothing to eat up there. And that coffee table is made of glass with sharp edges. And Justin's bottle cap collection." She paced the length of the kitchen and swiveled back around. "That place is a death trap for a young child. They'll have to stay here."

Ian watched in awe and with helpless appreciation as Jaci picked up the plan where he'd dead-ended.

"She can sleep on the pullout couch. I think Jena will enjoy having another mother around to keep her company. Heck, this place is already baby central. I hope Mandy can stand it." Jaci looked at him. "Why are you just sitting there? Go get her."

"You're not mad?"

Jaci looked down at him like he wasn't making sense. "Why would I be mad? Your friend's wife needs help and we're going to see that she gets it."

Ian walked over to Jaci and pulled her into his arms. "You are one of a kind special." He kissed her cheek.

"Remember that the next time I do something that pisses you off." She rested her head against his chest and squeezed him back. "Oh. And for the record? You're pretty special yourself."

CHAPTER TEN

Jaci ended the phone call and looked at her watch. Again. Eight-thirteen. She'd been waiting almost half an hour. Now she'd have to double time it to complete her patient visits and get to the crisis center in time for her baby care class.

Eight-thirteen.

Too early for the criminal element to be up and about. She scanned the front grounds of Nap Tower, mostly cement and packed dirt. An old woman pushed a cart toward Jaci's car. Two young children, one in a pink windbreaker, one in blue, chased pigeons while a heavy set black woman sat on a bench nearby talking into a cell phone.

Jaci got out of the car.

What would Ian want me to do in this situation? She smiled. *So I can return home to him safe and sound and he can reward me by doing wonderfully erotic things to my body.* She opened the rear door and grabbed her nursing bag.

Then she dialed Ian.

"Are you okay?" he asked in greeting.

"Fine." She started toward the entrance. "My police escort got called to a shooting and there is no one in the area to accompany me on a quick visit to change an IV at Nap Tower."

"I can be there in twenty minutes."

"In twenty minutes, I'll be done."

"Do not go in there alone," he warned.

"I'm not." She opened the heavy glass door trying not to think about the bullet that caused the hole and spider webbed cracks. "You're accompanying me." She opened the metal door to the stairwell and listened. Hearing voices, she opted for the elevator. "It's early. There aren't many people around."

"I don't like this."

"Elevator's here." She looked inside. "It's empty so I'm going in. If I lose you don't panic. I'll call you when I get to the second floor." She exited. "You still there?"

"I'm here." But he didn't sound at all happy. "From now on whenever you have to do visits there I'll plan to meet you."

"We can talk about it later." She walked down the dingy hallway, the air heavy with the scent of frying oil, and knocked on the door with a two, an eight, and a backwards three. "I'm here." Her patient's husband opened the door. She gave him a smile and a wave. "Safe and sound." She walked inside. "I'll call you when I'm ready to leave."

And she'd planned to, except twenty minutes later she had an emergency call from her office and was on the phone with her supervisor as she prepared to leave. She pressed the downward arrow next to the elevator.

The doors opened. This time the elevator was not empty. And Oh. My. God. There stood Merlene's boyfriend. Still in his uniform. Coming home from his job on the night shift. And he looked straight at her.

Jaci diverted her eyes. "I'll be down in a minute. I'm

getting on the elevator now," she said to make it seem like someone was waiting for her in the lobby.

But her voice shook.

"What's wrong?" her supervisor asked.

Merlene's boyfriend exited the elevator and she entered. "Breakfast sounds great," she said to make conversation.

Then she felt a hulking presence behind her.

"Been waiting for the day you and me would meet up," Merlene's boyfriend said deeply, quietly. Threateningly.

Jaci whipped around. He had her cornered, his large body blocking her escape. He pressed a button on the control panel and the doors started to close. "Call the police," she yelled into her phone. He slapped it out of her hand. "Help," she screamed as loud as she could, hoping someone would come to her aid.

No one did.

The doors closed.

She was trapped.

He triggered the emergency stop and the elevator jerked to a halt. The alarm blared.

He took a step forward.

Jaci backed into the rear wall of the tiny elevator, regretting that she'd never told Ian she loved him, knowing in her heart if she didn't make it out alive, he'd look after Jena and the babies. Because he was a good man. The very best kind of man.

Ian glanced at the clock in his office. Eight forty-five. And he hadn't heard from Jaci. He texted her. So what if she got mad. She was the one who'd said she'd call him when she was done.

When she didn't respond in five minutes, unease

crept up his spine, making him restless. He curbed the urge to jump in the car and drive down to Nap Tower. Jaci was a grown woman, he told himself. She could take care of herself. He had to learn to trust her judgment.

He grabbed his tool belt and headed to the kitchen to replace the drippy faucet. There must be a perfectly reasonable explanation for why she hadn't taken the time for a quick reply.

Ian would not obsess over it.

He got to work, thankful for a busy schedule of repairs ahead of him, already looking forward to three o'clock when Jaci would arrive with a smile, ready for her baby care class.

A while later Andrea found him at the back door, in the middle of installing a heavy duty deadbolt lock. So what if the parking lot had an aging fence around it, anyone with working arms and legs could climb over in under a minute.

"Mr. Eddelton? Are you busy?"

Had it been anyone else he may have shot back, "Do I look busy?" On his knees, tools and lock parts spread out on the floor around him, the not-as-easy-as-they'd-promised instruction sheet in hand. But it was timid, conscientious Andrea, who Ian had learned was one of the first clients of the center. He stopped what he was doing. "What do you need?"

"I stepped away from the phone for a very quick break." She pushed her glasses up on the bridge of her nose. "I had to use the restroom, but I went right back to my desk when I was done." She rubbed her hands together nervously. "I'm afraid in that very short time Ms. Piermont called and left a message for Carla."

"Ms. Piermont doesn't expect you to be chained to your desk for the entire time you're here. I'm sure—"

"You don't understand. Carla's son is sick. She had to take him to the doctor this morning. And even though Ms. Piermont left specific instructions not to worry you, I think something's very wrong."

Ian set down his screwdriver and stood, his unease multiplying exponentially.

"I heard it in her voice, Mr. Eddelton." She looked up almost in tears. "I need this job. If I go against Ms. Piermont's instructions again—"

"What did she say in the message?" Panic rising, Ian fought for calm.

"She asked Carla to meet her at the Emergency Room at Sound Shore Medical Center."

Ian slammed the door closed and engaged the old lock. "Did she say why?" he asked over his shoulder on his way to his office to get his keys.

"No." Andrea half-ran half-walked behind him, crying.

He didn't have time to console her. "Call Carla's cellphone. Tell her about the message and that I'm on my way to the hospital. Find Patrice," their social worker. "Tell her what's going on. Make sure she knows she's in charge. Anyone makes you nervous, don't buzz them in." The front door and entry intercom were the first things he'd fixed.

Ian didn't remember the trip to the hospital, wasn't sure how much time had passed. He slammed his SUV into park, left it at the curb and ran through the sliding glass doors into the Emergency Room. "Jaci Piermont," he said to the first scrub-clad staff person he saw.

"You don't look like a Carla," a heavyset, no-nonsense nurse said from behind the nurses' station. "I am under strict instructions to only provide information to a Carla."

Rage and desperation pounded through his system. To hell with counting and deep breathing and exercising. "I am Jaci Piermont's fiancé." Though he wasn't yet, he would be soon. And once they were married he planned to fill her with so many babies she'd be too busy to leave the house.

"Well you can go wait with the other fiancés in the waiting room." She waved him away and turned her attention to the computer monitor in front of her. "You reporters will do anything for a story."

Ian walked to the desk. "I am Ian Eddelton," he said slowly so there'd be no mistake. "Jaci and I have just recently been reunited after being separated for thirteen months because of the war." He moderated his tone so as not to sound like a man about to wreak havoc until he found her.

The nurse looked over his upper body and still-military-short haircut.

Ian's control started to slip. He leaned over the top of the counter. "Now, either you tell me where she is or you're going to need a hell of a lot more manpower than that scrawny security guard over there to keep me from searching every single room." Ian turned down the hallway. "Jaci," he called out. "Jaci," he yelled even louder.

"Calm down. Calm down." The nurse heaved herself out of her chair. "Wait here and keep quiet, for heaven's sake. Give me a minute to talk to my patient."

Ian watched her knock on a door halfway down the hall. As soon as she entered, he followed her.

At his appearance the nurse said, "He doesn't listen very well."

Jaci sat in a chair in the far corner of the small private

exam room, wearing a hospital gown, her eyes red and swollen shut, an oxygen mask hanging around her neck.

"He said he was my fiancé?" Jaci asked, her voice hoarse. Raw.

His heart squeezed. He couldn't expand his lungs. Had she been beaten? Choked? Worse?

"Ian Eddelton," the nurse said.

"Please don't yell at me, Ian," she said, turning her head away and inhaling a shaky breath. "I really can't handle being yelled at right now."

"What happened?" he asked quietly as he walked to her.

She didn't answer.

Ian pulled the guest chair beside her, sat down, and tugged on her hand to see if she'd come to him. As if the seat beneath her had an eject feature, Jaci launched herself at his chest and Ian held her while she cried. No matter what she'd been through, he'd help her deal with it. They'd help each other.

"I'll be at the desk if you need me Ms. Piermont," the nurse said. "Buzzer's clipped to your gown."

"Th-thank you," Jaci said, sniffling.

Finally alone in the room Ian smoothed Jaci's wild curls and said, "I know how difficult it is to talk about some things." It'd been months since the bomb blast and he still wasn't able to discuss certain details. "But you're the one who said women like to talk and my imagination is a scary place so I am praying you'll take pity on me and tell me what happened to you." Please, Lord, grant him the strength to take it like a man and remain strong for her. "Whatever it is, we'll get through it. Together."

"You were right," she said. "My luck ran out. Just like you said it would."

That was the absolute last thing Ian wanted to be

right about. He wanted to shout out his anger. At her for not waiting for him to accompany her into that cursed building. At himself for not listening to the feeling of unease he'd experienced earlier, similar to the one he'd experienced on the morning of that fateful night four months ago. But what good would it do now? He rubbed her back to calm her.

"In the elevator."

Ian's breakfast churned in his stomach.

"After my visit, I was on the phone with my supervisor. That's why I didn't call you. I met up with Merlene's boyfriend at the elevator. He got off so I thought I was okay. But he doubled back in behind me."

That beast had a good foot on Jaci and at least one hundred pounds. Ian saw red. His vision a slo-mo enactment of all the ways he would torture that animal when he found him. And he would find him. Ten. Nine. Eight. Seven. Six.

"Breathe," she said, tapping on his chest.

So focused on counting to counteract his rage, he'd completely forgotten that life-sustaining necessity. Ian's imagination turned to Jaci. Lying on the elevator floor. His heart pounded. Gorge worked its way up to the back of his throat.

"It's not what you think," Jaci said, saving him from a complete psychotic meltdown.

"He trapped me in there but he didn't touch me."

Thank you, God. Tears of relief pooled in Ian's eyes. He squeezed her tight and kissed the top of her head. "Then what happened to your eyes?"

"He hit the emergency stop button and cornered me. He threatened me and waved a knife around, wanting me to take him to Merlene."

"Why—?"

"I know if I did, you would have been there and taken care of him." She twisted a button on his shirt. "But I had to think of Merlene and her baby. She's been running hypertensive. Any stress would put additional strain on her already high-risk pregnancy."

That's what Jaci did. She put the people she cared about before herself. As much as he'd like to scream at her to stop it, her caring and compassion were two of the many reasons he loved her. And Ian realized as hard as he tried, he couldn't change Jaci from being…Jaci. He could and would continue to urge caution, suggest alternative action, and do his best to protect her, but she'd go right on doing what was innately part of her character. If he wanted a future with Jaci, and he did, he needed to give her freedom to live her life, trust so she'd trust him in return, and support when she got into trouble.

He said a quick prayer on everything holy that today was the worst of it.

"So what did you do?"

"As the minutes passed he became more agitated. I tried to rationalize with him, but he wouldn't listen. He threatened to scar me or take *me* to replace Merlene." She shivered. Ian tightened his hold on her to remind her she was safe.

"I kept my hand in my pocket the entire time. When he made a lunge to grab me, I blasted him in the eyes with pepper spray."

Jaci had more courage than some soldiers he'd served with over the years.

"He dropped to the ground, screaming and writhing, according to plan. But the noxious plume affected me, too. I barely reached the panel to get the elevator moving before my eyes swelled shut. It hurt so bad, like my eyes, nasal passages and face were on fire."

Unfortunately, Ian was familiar with that "on fire" feeling.

"The doors opened on the second floor where my patient's husband was waiting. He pulled the fire alarm to summon help and absolute chaos ensued. I'm told a television news van had been in the area doing a story on the local teen who'd been shot this morning. My nurse says reporters have been calling and showing up since I got here." She shrugged. "I guess my secret life as a home health care nurse is no longer secret."

Good. Maybe now she'd focus her attentions on the crisis center, where he could keep an eye on her.

"I'm so glad you came." She snuggled into his chest.

"Even though you didn't want me here." Which stung.

"I worried about how you'd handle it. I can't very well calm *you* down when *I'm* totally freaked out. I can't see. Merlene's boyfriend was brought to the hospital, too. He's here somewhere. What's to stop him from coming in here to follow through on his threats?" She tried to burrow deeper into his chest.

"Me." He hugged her, hoping the son-of-a-bitch would show himself so Ian could mete out some retaliation in a fair fight between two comparable opponents. Man to man. Not vicious bully to woman.

No. Nix the war mentality. Violence was not the answer. He channeled his anger management. Ten. Inhale. Exhale. Nine. Inhale. Exhale.

Think happy thoughts. Merlene's boyfriend standing on a tenth floor ledge facing the shooting end of Ian's firearm. Good. Well, it worked for Ian, but his therapist probably would not approve.

He tried again. Jaci in her oversized tub. Naked. Surrounded by bubbles. Candlelight. An invitation to join her. Better.

Already feeling calmer, Ian decided one more happy thought should do it. He had survived three tours of duty in Iraq. He knew several dozen soldiers who couldn't say the same. He had four women and seven children depending on him to be around for them. He had Jaci and Jena and the twins and Justin. He had a full life, a promising future, and no intention of wasting either by serving time in prison for manslaughter. Best.

Ian would let the law handle Merlene's boyfriend.

The nurse returned. "The doctor wants me to clean your eyes out again before he examines you for discharge."

Jaci felt down his arm to his hand and threaded her fingers through his. "Will you stay?"

He kissed the top of her head. "Try getting rid of me."

CHAPTER ELEVEN

"Where's Jena and Mandy?" Ian asked later that afternoon when he returned to her bedroom after being gone for several hours.

At the sound of his voice Jaci's spirits lifted instantly.

She forced open her still swollen eyelids. He was literally a wonderful sight for sore eyes. "They took the babies out to give me some quiet," Jaci said, patting the bed beside her. It hadn't been easy to convince Jena to leave. "You were gone longer than I expected. Is everything okay at the center?"

"Fine." He sat down and pushed her hair behind her ear. "Carla made it in as soon as her mom came over to watch her son. We decided not to tell Merlene what happened."

"Good."

"Which meant I had to disable the cable TV in the common room so nobody heard about it on the news."

"Oh, man. Thank you. I hadn't even considered that."

"Carla broke out some board games, playing cards and books to ease the unrest. When I left a couple of hours ago, all was quiet."

A couple of hours? If he hadn't been at the center all this time, where was he while she lay in bed feeling sorry for herself and aching for his company and reliving the attack over and over? She shivered.

"Hey." He climbed over her and lay down to cuddle her back to his front. "You're okay."

She felt on the verge of tears. "I keep seeing…"

He held her close. "I know." He kissed the back of her head. "It will get better."

But when? "Where have you been?" That was more important than spending time with her?

"I had some errands to run. How do you feel?"

"Better. But bored. I'm not used to lying around doing nothing." And jumping at every noise. "My eyes start to ache if I keep them open for too long."

"I brought dinner and a movie. I chose a romantic comedy." He lifted her hand to his lips and kissed it. "I'll keep my eyes closed and we can listen to it together."

His thoughtfulness made her cry. "I don't know what's wrong with me." She blotted her tears on the sheet. "I'm so weepy."

"Traumatic day." He squeezed her hand.

"You've been wonderful." So supportive. Staying with her while the nurse treated her eyes then helping her dress to leave the hospital, paying a guy from the hospital laundry to sneak her out the back service entrance in a rolling bin so she didn't have to face the reporters then covering at the crisis center until Carla could get there.

But she needed one more thing. "Do you think…? I mean would you…?"

"Anything," Ian said.

"I think I'll go absolutely crazy if I have to lie in this bed, all by myself for the entire night. I keep seeing his face. His sneer. And the knife." She felt cold. "Will you stay with me tonight?" she asked.

"Every night," he said.

"Good answer."

They lay together quietly. After a while Jaci said, "When I was in that elevator, not sure if I'd make it out alive, you know the one regret that came to me?"

"What?"

"That I'd never told you I loved you."

"I love—"

"Don't." She held up a hand. "You don't have to say it just because I did." Not if he didn't mean it.

He cleared his throat. "When I was pinned beneath what was left of our Humvee, waiting to be rescued," he said. "Surrounded by gunfire outside and my men, my closest friends besides Justin, all dead inside, I thought about you. How sorry I was I'd never again get the chance to see your beautiful face, or hold you, or hear your laugh. That I wouldn't make it home to tell you, at some point during our friendship, or between us making love for the first time, me reading and rereading your letter, and fantasizing about your marriage proposal and us having a future together, I'd fallen in love with you. At least I'd thought I had."

"Nice," she said with what she hoped was the right amount of sarcasm.

"What I felt then is nothing compared to what I feel since getting to know the real you. I love you, Jaci and I want you in my life all day, every day until I take my last breath."

"Nice recovery," she teased.

"I'm serious. And I don't want to wait to get married," he added. "Life can be snuffed out in an instant." He rolled off the bed.

"Where are you going, now?"

"Remember I told you I had some errands to run? Well I stopped by my safety deposit box." He rustled through one of the bags he'd carried in earlier. "Here." he placed something in her palm. A ring. She strained to focus on it. Silver or white gold. Vintage. A brilliant, square, princess cut diamond, at least one carat. Probably more. Delicate filigree with two baguettes. Absolutely beautiful.

"That's an engagement ring," he said. "It belonged to my grandmother on my father's side. When you can see a little better you can tell me if you like it."

Like it? She loved it, especially that his grandmother had once worn it. But, "Is that your idea of a proposal?"

He thought about it. "What would you say if I said, yes?"

"I'd say, you think, 'Here. That's an engagement ring. When you can see a little better you can tell me if you like it' is a better proposal than, 'My God that was amazing. Please say you'll marry me?'"

He smiled then knelt down by the side of the bed, gripped the ring between his thumb and index finger and held it out to her. "Jaci Piermont, you make me happy. I love you and want to spend every day for the rest of my life with you and I want our time together as man and wife to start as soon as possible. Would you do me the honor of marrying me? And might I suggest you don't take too long to answer or I may need some assistance getting up from the floor."

Jaci didn't need to take any time at all. "I'd love to wear an Eddelton heirloom." She held out her left hand. He slipped the ring onto her ring finger and settled it at the base like it was made to be there. With absolute certainty she answered, "And I'd love to marry you."

Ian leaned in and kissed her then stood and joined her back on the bed. "While I was out, I also had a pre-nuptial agreement drawn up."

Jaci started to argue but he held a finger to her lips. "Sign it, don't sign it. It's completely up to you. Your money is yours to do with as you choose. If you'd like us to officially marry before your birthday so you can claim your trust or if you'd like to hold off, is completely up to you. As far as I'm concerned, by accepting my ring we're joined together by love, respect, and honor. You are my wife in my heart as of today, and that's all that matters to me."

Ian almost dying in the war and the altercation with Merlene's boyfriend really hit home the fact that each day of life was a precious gift not to be squandered on indecision and delay in pursuing your heart's desire. "What would you say to a Las Vegas wedding as soon as I can make the travel arrangements?"

"I'd say let me boot up your laptop then I'll help you pack." But the kiss he planted on her lips was not from a man intent on searching the Internet any time soon.

When they broke for air Jaci said, "You know how you said my money is mine to do with as I choose?"

Ian nodded.

"Well, with the first trust fund check I plan to set up seven fifty-thousand-dollar college savings accounts for the children of your men, to honor their memory and their service and dedication to our country."

Ian's next kiss conveyed without words just how much he liked and appreciated the idea. It was the least she could do. "And while we're on the topic of children, maybe we could talk about babies?"

Ian rolled onto his back, taking Jaci with him to rest on his chest. "What about them?"

"I want some." She straddled his groin.

"When were you looking to have them?" He squeezed her butt, pressed down, and rocked his pelvis up between her legs.

Ah, yes. A future filled with Ian—literally and figuratively—was a bright one indeed. "How does nine months sound?" So Jena's babies and her babies would be close in age.

"Like we'd better get started." He had her pajama top halfway off when he hesitated.

"Are you sure you're up for it."

Jaci pushed herself upright, went onto her knees, and slid his hand under the elastic of her lounge pants. He moved the rest of the way on his own, slipping along her slick folds, plunging two fingers deep inside her.

"I guess that's a yes," he said with a big smile.

Jaci reached down to caress his erection through his slacks. "And you're definitely up for it." Jaci returned his smile.

"Yes, ma'am," Ian said, placing his hands on her hips and applying downward pressure. "Awaiting orders, ma'am," he added with a seductive grin as he lifted his hips to meet her.

He wanted orders? She'd give him orders. "Love me," she said, looking deep into his eyes. "Make me yours."

And Ian did just that.

* * * * *

ROMANCE

MEDICAL

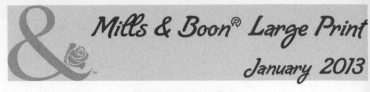

ROMANCE

Unlocking her Innocence	Lynne Graham
Santiago's Command	Kim Lawrence
His Reputation Precedes Him	Carole Mortimer
The Price of Retribution	Sara Craven
The Valtieri Baby	Caroline Anderson
Slow Dance with the Sheriff	Nikki Logan
Bella's Impossible Boss	Michelle Douglas
The Tycoon's Secret Daughter	Susan Meier
Just One Last Night	Helen Brooks
The Greek's Acquisition	Chantelle Shaw
The Husband She Never Knew	Kate Hewitt

HISTORICAL

His Mask of Retribution	Margaret McPhee
How to Disgrace a Lady	Bronwyn Scott
The Captain's Courtesan	Lucy Ashford
Man Behind the Façade	June Francis
The Highlander's Stolen Touch	Terri Brisbin

MEDICAL

Sydney Harbour Hospital: Marco's Temptation	Fiona McArthur
Waking Up With His Runaway Bride	Louisa George
The Legendary Playboy Surgeon	Alison Roberts
Falling for Her Impossible Boss	Alison Roberts
Letting Go With Dr Rodriguez	Fiona Lowe
Dr Tall, Dark...and Dangerous?	Lynne Marshall

ROMANCE

Sold to the Enemy	Sarah Morgan
Uncovering the Silveri Secret	Melanie Milburne
Bartering Her Innocence	Trish Morey
Dealing Her Final Card	Jennie Lucas
In the Heat of the Spotlight	Kate Hewitt
No More Sweet Surrender	Caitlin Crews
Pride After Her Fall	Lucy Ellis
Living the Charade	Michelle Conder
The Downfall of a Good Girl	Kimberly Lang
The One That Got Away	Kelly Hunter
Her Rocky Mountain Protector	Patricia Thayer
The Billionaire's Baby SOS	Susan Meier
Baby out of the Blue	Rebecca Winters
Ballroom to Bride and Groom	Kate Hardy
How To Get Over Your Ex	Nikki Logan
Must Like Kids	Jackie Braun
The Brooding Doc's Redemption	Kate Hardy
The Son that Changed his Life	Jennifer Taylor

MEDICAL

An Inescapable Temptation	Scarlet Wilson
Revealing The Real Dr Robinson	Dianne Drake
The Rebel and Miss Jones	Annie Claydon
Swallowbrook's Wedding of the Year	Abigail Gordon

Mills & Boon® Large Print

February 2013

ROMANCE

HISTORICAL

MEDICAL